A Slight Misunderstanding

Prosper Mérimée

Translated by Douglas Parmée

ONEWORLD
CLASSICS

ONEWORLD CLASSICS LTD
London House
243-253 Lower Mortlake Road
Richmond
Surrey TW9 2LL
United Kingdom
www.oneworldclassics.com

A Slight Misunderstanding first published in 1833

Translation © John Calder (Publishers) Limited, 1959
First published in this translation from the French 1959 by John Calder (Publishers) Limited
This edition first published by Oneworld Classics Limited in 2008
Reprinted 2009, 2011

Front cover image © Getty Images

Printed in Great Britain by CPI Antony Rowe

ISBN: 978-1-84749-076-6

Contents

Introduction

Prosper Mérimée is widely known as the author of the admirable short stories *Colomba* and *Carmen*, where primitive passions work themselves out against a colourful background of Corsican banditry and Spanish gypsy life. A different Mérimée, however, the friend and admirer of Stendhal and Sainte-Beuve, is seen in a number of stories where, eschewing facile exotic effects, he takes us into the Parisian *mondaine* society of his day and while revealing some of its general habits and customs, acutely analyses a few of its individual members.

Of such stories, *La Double Méprise* is undoubtedly the masterpiece. It was first published in 1833, when Mérimée, at the age of thirty, having lived for some ten years the life of a Parisian man-about-town, was in a good position to know his subject thoroughly. In no other work does he so well combine witty and accurate social observation with acute psychological insight. The plot is simple, if not banal; but in this account of an unhappy wife's adultery, Mérimée has contrived to include a great variety of moods and the action

1

is the more dramatic, the impact all the greater by reason of the author's restricted canvas. In a few score pages, we are aroused to sympathy, not unalloyed with exasperation, at Julie's marriage, we are irritated and appalled by her husband, diverted and antagonized by her suitor, regaled by scenes at the Opera and in a *salon*, entertained by an exotic, mock-heroic adventure, seized and disturbed by the drama of Julie's encounter with Darcy, shocked and moved by its brutal dénouement and harrowed by her pathetic, indeed tragic fate. All this is achieved with great economy – a passing comment, a suggestive detail, a gesture, a word – as well as by most careful construction; and we are left with an indelible impression of the complexities and ironies of love in the modern world. To take two extreme examples, nothing could be more comical yet pathetic than Chaverny's vain attempts at making love to his wife, having forgotten how to do so; on the other hand, the skilfully prepared dramatic meeting of Julie and Darcy leads on to the extraordinary tenseness of emotion of the carefully observed seduction in the carriage.

In view of this, it is less surprising than might appear to those unfamiliar with this work that some years ago a distinguished committee of well-known French authors and critics, in choosing the twelve best novels of the nineteenth century, included in them *La Double Méprise*. It is, indeed, rather more surprising that this masterpiece should be relatively unknown in England.

Douglas Parmée

Queens' College, Cambridge

1958

Chronological Table of Mérimée's Life

1803   Mérimée born in Paris on 28th September.

1823   Completes his legal studies at Paris University.

1823–33 Active social and literary life in Paris, friendship
with Stendhal and Ampère.

1825   Publication of *Théâtre de Clara Gazul*, sup-
posedly a translation from the Spanish, in reality his
own work.

1826   First of many visits to England, where he had
numerous friends.

1827   Publication of *Guzla*, a pastiche of Serbian folk
ballads.

1828   Publication of *La Jacquerie*, a work on the
Peasants' Revolt in France.

1829   Publication of the *Chronique du Règne de
Charles IX*, an historical novel about the Massacre of
St Bartholomew's day.

1829–30 Publication of Mérimée's first short stories:
Mateo Falcone, *L'Enlèvement de la Redoute*, *Tamango*,
Le Vase Etrusque, *La Partie de Trictrac*.

5

1830	First of many trips to Spain.
1833	Publication of *La Double Méprise*.
1834	Appointed Inspector General of Historical Monuments, in which capacity he travelled during the next eighteen years all over France.
1837	Publication of *La Vénus d'Ille*.
1839	Visit to Corsica and Italy.
1840	Publication of *Colomba*; long trip to Spain.
1841	Visit to Italy, Greece, Asia Minor and Turkey.
1844	Publication of *Arsène Guillot*.
1845	Publication of *Carmen*; Mérimée becomes a member of the French Academy.
1848	Mérimée starts to learn Russian and in the ensuing years publishes a number of translations and studies of the works of Pushkin, Gogol, Turgenyev, etc.
1853	Mérimée becomes a Senator and frequents the court circles of Napoleon III; friendship with Sainte-Beuve.
1870	Mérimée dies in Cannes on 3rd September.

A Slight Misunderstanding

1

Zagala, mas que las flores Blanca, rubia y ojos verdes, Si piensas seguir amores Piérdete bien, pues te pierdes.

MARRIED SOME SIX YEARS AGO, Julie de Chaverny had now known for approximately the last five years and six months that it was not only impossible to love her husband but difficult even to feel any respect for him. Not that her husband was offensive, nor was he either foolish or stupid. And yet perhaps he was something of all three. Looking back, she might have recalled having once liked him; now, he bored her. She found everything about him repellent: the way he ate, the way he drank his coffee, the way he spoke, set her nerves on edge. They hardly ever saw or spoke to each other except at table; but as they dined together a number of times a week, this was quite enough to keep her aversion alive.

As for Chaverny, he was not bad-looking, a trifle stout for his age, with a fresh, ruddy face and a temperament which protected him from those vague yearnings that so often afflict people with imagination. He held the pious belief that his wife had a gentle affection for him (being too worldly-wise to imagine

9

that she loved him as much as when they were married); and this conviction caused him neither grief nor joy; the reverse would have been just as acceptable. He had served for several years in the cavalry but having come into a great deal of money, he tired of garrison life, resigned his commission and married. It may seem somewhat difficult to explain why two people who had not a single idea in common should have married. On one hand, grandparents and those other busybodies who, like Phrosyne, would have married off the Republic of Venice to the Great Turk, had gone to a good deal of trouble to settle the business side. On the other, Chaverny came of good family; he was not, at that time, too fat; he was high-spirited and in every sense of the word what is known as a good sort. Julie was always glad to see him when he called on her mother because he told stories about his regiment which were funny as well as slightly improper. She liked him because he was always ready to dance with her at the various balls and always found some good reason to persuade Julie's mother not to go home too early or else to go to the theatre or the Bois de Boulogne. Above all, Julie thought him a hero because he had acquitted himself honourably in a couple of duels. What finally won her heart, however, was his description of a special carriage he was going to have built according to his own specification and in which he personally was going to take Julie driving once she had agreed to be his wife.

After a few months of married life, Chaverny's qualities had all lost much of their lustre. He had, of course, stopped dancing with his wife. He always complained, now, that dances went on too long. He had told all his funny stories half a dozen times. At the theatre he yawned continually, and thought dressing for dinner an intolerable imposition. His chief fault was that he was lazy; had he made the effort to be agreeable, he might perhaps have succeeded, but he found any sort of compulsion unbearable – a common fault with most fat people. Society bored him because you are only welcome in it if you are prepared to make an effort to be agreeable. In fact, his amusements were rather more broad than refined, for in order to make his presence felt in the sort of company he liked, all he had to do was to shout louder than anyone else, which was not difficult as he had very powerful lungs. In addition, he prided himself on being able to drink more champagne than most people and could jump his horse over a five-barred gate with the greatest elegance. As a result, he enjoyed the legitimate respect of those people, difficult to define, who are called young men-about-town and who are to be seen on the boulevards at about five o'clock every evening. He was very keen on shooting parties, picnics, the races, bachelor dinners and supper parties. A dozen times a day he would say he was the happiest man alive and every time Julie heard him, she would raise her eyes to heaven and her tiny mouth took on an expression of unutterable scorn.

Young, beautiful and married to a man whom she disliked, one may imagine that she was bound to be surrounded by much admiration which was far from disinterested. But in addition to the protection afforded by her mother, an extremely cautious woman, her pride, which was her great weakness, had hitherto prevented her being led astray by the society in which she moved. In any case, the disappointment caused by her marriage, whilst giving her a sort of worldly wisdom, had clipped the wings of her enthusiasms. She was gratified to find herself an object of sympathy amongst her friends and quoted by them as a paragon of self-sacrifice. And after all, she was almost happy, for she was not in love with anyone and her husband left her completely free to do as she pleased. If she flirted (and it must be confessed that she was not averse from proving that her husband did not know what a treasure he possessed), if she flirted it was instinctively, like a child, and her flirtatiousness was not incompatible with a certain disdainful aloofness, although she was not prudish. In a word, she knew the art of being agreeable to everybody in general and to no one in particular. She had never given the least grounds for gossip.

2

HUSBAND AND WIFE had dined with Julie's mother, Mme de Lussan, who was leaving shortly for Nice. Chaverny, who was always desperately bored at his mother-in-law's, had found himself obliged to spend the evening there, in spite of his strong desire to go and join his friends on the boulevard. After dinner, he had settled down on a comfortable settee and not said a word for a couple of hours. The reason for this was simple: he was asleep, observing the decencies, of course, with his head on one side, as if following the conversation with interest; even, now and again, he woke up and passed a remark.

Later, he was unable to refuse a game of whist – a game which he loathed because it requires a certain concentration. All this meant that it was now rather late: half-past eleven had just struck. Chaverny had no engagements that evening and he had not the slightest idea of what to do. Whilst he was puzzling over this problem, the carriage was announced. If he went home, his wife would have to go with him. The prospect of being alone with her for twenty minutes was alarming; but he had forgotten his cigars and he was longing to open a box of them which had been delivered just as he was leaving for dinner. He decided to make the best of it.

As he was helping his wife into her wrap, he could not help smiling at his reflection in the mirror: he looked like a man just recently married. He also saw his wife, whom he normally never looked at. That evening she seemed rather prettier than usual and so he lingered over arranging the shawl over her shoulders. Julie was just as vexed as he was over the impending tête-à-tête with her husband. She was pouting and unconsciously puckering her arched eyebrows. This made her look so charming that even a husband could hardly remain unmoved. During the operation which I have described, their eyes met in the mirror. They were both embarrassed. To recover his self-possession, Chaverny smiled and kissed his wife's hand as she raised it to adjust her shawl.

"How they love each other!" murmured Mme de Lussan to herself, failing to notice her daughter's cold disdain or the husband's casual air.

When they were alone together in their carriage, sitting almost touching, they did not speak at first. True, Chaverny felt he ought to say something but he couldn't, for the life of him, think what to say. Julie for her part was grimly silent. He yawned three or four times and the last time, even ashamed himself, he felt bound to apologize.

"It was a long evening," he added as an excuse. Julie considered this last remark as deliberately calculated to disparage her mother's dinner parties and be unpleasant to herself, but she had long since reached the stage of avoiding any discussion with her husband. She continued to remain silent.

Chaverny, in spite of himself, felt communicative that evening and after a couple of minutes, he went on:

"As a matter of fact, it was quite a good meal this evening but I'm pleased to tell you that your mother's champagne is too sweet."

"What did you say?" asked Julie, turning towards him with marked unconcern and pretending not to have been listening.

"I was saying that your mother's champagne is too sweet. I forgot to mention it to her. It's an amazing thing but people imagine that it's easy to choose champagne. In fact, there's nothing harder. There are twenty sorts of bad champagne and only one that's any good."

"Really?" And Julie, after this concession to good manners, turned away and looked out of the window on her side. Chaverny lounged back and put his feet on the seat opposite, a trifle mortified at his wife's indifference to all his efforts to start a conversation.

However, two or three yawns later, he drew closer to Julie and went on:

"That dress you're wearing suits you perfectly, Julie. Where did you buy it?"

"I suppose he wants to buy one like it for his mistress," thought Julie. Aloud, with a slight smile: "I got it from Burty's."

"What are you laughing at?" asked Chaverny, removing his feet from the seat and moving even closer. At the same time, he took hold of one of the sleeves of her dress and started playing with it.

"I'm laughing," said Julie, "because you noticed what I'm wearing. Be careful, you're crumpling my sleeves." And she pulled her sleeve out of Chaverny's hand.

"I assure you, I pay a lot of attention to what you wear and I admire your taste tremendously. No, honestly, only the other day I was talking about it to... a woman who always dresses badly, although she spends a vast amount on clothes... She could easily ruin... I was telling her... I was quoting you..."

Julie, enjoying his embarrassment, made no attempt to interrupt him.

"What awful horses you have," said Chaverny, completely flustered. "They go so badly. I'll have to get you some others."

For the rest of the journey, conversation flagged; both confined themselves to commonplaces.

Eventually, they reached rue *** and parted after wishing each other good night.

Julie had started to undress and her maid had just gone out for something, when quite suddenly the bedroom door opened and in walked Chaverny. Julie hastily flung something over her shoulders.

"Excuse me," he said, "I'd rather like the last volume of Scott to send me to sleep… Isn't it *Quentin Durward?*"

"It must be in your room," said Julie, "there aren't any books here."

Chaverny was eyeing his wife whose dress was in that state of slight disorder which is so attractive. He found her rather "piquant" (if I may use an expression I detest). "She's really a very lovely woman," he was thinking to himself. And, candle in hand, he stood there in front of her, not moving or saying a word. Julie, also standing facing him, was nervously crumpling her nightcap in one hand and seemed to be waiting impatiently for him to leave her.

"You're charming tonight, I'm damned if you're not," exclaimed Chaverny, at length, taking a step forwards and putting down his candle. "How I love women with their hair down." So saying, with one hand he took hold of the long tresses that were covering her shoulders and, almost tenderly, slipped one arm round her waist.

"Heavens, what a dreadful smell of tobacco!" cried Julie,

drawing away. "Leave my hair alone, you'll impregnate it with the smell and I shan't be able to get it out."

"Now, now, you're just saying that because you know I sometimes smoke. Don't be so fussy, my sweetheart."

And she was unable to free herself quickly enough to avoid a kiss on her shoulder.

Fortunately for Julie, her maid came in; for there is nothing more odious to a woman than being fondled when she feels it equally as absurd to refuse as to accept.

"Marie," she said, "the bodice of my blue dress is much too long. I saw Mme de Bégy today who's always perfectly dressed and her bodice was certainly a good inch shorter. Now just take in a tuck here straight away so that we can see how it looks."

At this point, there took place a most interesting dialogue between the maid and her mistress on the exact dimensions of a bodice. Julie knew very well that her husband disliked nothing more than listening to talk about clothes and that she would soon send him packing. And so, after five minutes of bustling here and there, Chaverny, seeing that Julie was completely taken up with her bodice, yawned in a most terrifying manner, took up his candlestick and left, this time for good.

3

MAJOR PERRIN WAS SITTING at a little table, busily reading. His well-brushed coat, his cap and, above all, his posture, stiff as a ramrod, proclaimed him to be an old soldier. Everything in his room was spotless, but extremely simple. An inkwell and two quills already cut were on the table beside a pile of writing paper, not one sheet of which had been used for at least a year. If Major Perrin didn't write, he at least made up for it by reading a great deal. At the moment, he was reading Montesquieu's *Persian Letters* whilst smoking his meerschaum pipe and these two occupations had so engrossed him that at first he did not notice the entrance of Major de Châteaufort. He was a young officer from his own regiment, with a charming face, extremely likeable, somewhat conceited, a protégé of the Minister for War; in a word, the opposite of Major Perrin in almost every respect. Yet, quite unaccountably, they were great friends and saw each other every day.

Châteaufort tapped Major Perrin on the shoulder. The latter turned his head without removing his pipe from his mouth. His first reaction was one of pleasure at seeing his friend; his second, poor man, was sorrow at having to stop reading; his third showed that he had accepted the situation and would do his duty as host to the best of his ability. He fumbled in his pocket for the key of the cupboard containing a precious box of cigars which he didn't smoke himself and which he was doling out to his friend one by one; but Châteaufort, who had seen him do this a hundred times before, exclaimed: "No, don't, Perrin old man, keep your cigars. I've got some myself!" Then, from an elegant Mexican straw case he drew out a cinnamon-coloured cigar tapered at both ends, lit it and sprawled full-length on a small settee which Major Perrin never used, his head on a cushion and his feet up on the opposite end. Châteaufort first of all surrounded himself in a cloud of smoke and with his eyes shut seemed to be meditating on what he had to say. His face was beaming with joy and he seemed scarcely able to contain the secret which he was dying to divulge. Major Perrin, placing his chair opposite the settee, went on smoking for a while without saying anything; then, as Châteaufort seemed in no hurry to speak, he asked:

"How's Ourika?"

Ourika was a black mare which Châteaufort had been riding rather too hard and she was showing signs of becoming broken-winded.

"Very well," said Châteaufort, without hearing the question. "Perrin," he exclaimed, lifting his leg from the arm of the settee and pointing it towards him, "do you appreciate how lucky you are to be a friend of mine?"

The old Major searched round in his mind for all the benefits accruing from his acquaintance with Châteaufort and could only recall the gift of a pound or two of tobacco and a few days' confinement to barracks for being concerned in a duel in which Châteaufort had played the principal role. True, his friend had shown him many proofs of his trust: it was always he whom Châteaufort approached when he wanted someone to stand in as orderly officer or act as his second.

Châteaufort did not keep him searching long and held out a short note on satin-finished paper, made in England, covered in charming spidery handwriting. Major Perrin pulled a face, which was his equivalent of a smile. He had more than once seen satin-finished letters in a scrawly hand addressed to his friend.

"Here," said the latter, "read this and be grateful to me."

Perrin read as follows:

We should be delighted, my dear Major de Châteaufort, if you will do us the pleasure of coming to dinner with us. M. de Chaverny would have come and asked you himself but he has had to leave for a shooting party. I don't know Major Perrin's address and so cannot write to ask him to come with you. You have made me very anxious to meet him and I shall be doubly grateful if you can bring him along with you.

Julie de Chaverny

P.S. I am greatly obliged to you for the music you took the trouble to copy out for me. It is absolutely delightful and I admire your taste very much. Have you given up coming on Thursdays? Surely you know how delighted we always are to see you.

"Pretty handwriting but too small," remarked Perrin, finishing the letter. "Drat it, anyway. Her dinner's a bore, because it'll mean silk stockings and no smoking after dinner."

"What a terrible calamity! Fancy preferring your pipe to the prettiest woman in Paris. But what I really appreciate is your lack of gratitude. You haven't even thanked me for this pleasant surprise I've brought you."

"Not thanked you, indeed! But it's not you I have to thank for this favour… if it is a favour."

"Whom then?"

"Why, Chaverny, who was one of my captains. No doubt he's told his wife: 'Ask Perrin, he's a good sort'. Otherwise, how on earth could a pretty young woman, whom I've only met once, anyway, think of asking an old ranker like me?"

Châteaufort smiled at himself in the narrow mirror which adorned the major's room.

"You're not very bright today, uncle Perrin. Just read this note again and perhaps you'll find something you missed."

The major turned the letter in all directions but in vain.

"Why, you old sweat," cried Châteaufort, "can't you see she's inviting you just to please me, to show she appreciates my friends?... She wants to prove..."

"Prove what?" interrupted Perrin.

"You know well enough what."

"That she loves you?" enquired the major with a dubious air.

Châteaufort's only reply was a whistle.

"So she's in love with you?"

Châteaufort went on whistling.

"She's told you so?"

"But... it's obvious, it seems to me."

"What? In that letter?"

"Of course."

It was Perrin's turn to whistle – a whistle as full of meaning as Uncle Toby's "Lillibulero".

"What!" cried Châteaufort, snatching the letter out of Perrin's hands. "Do you mean you can't see all the... fondness... yes, fondness is the word... in that letter? What do you say to this: *My dear Major de Châteaufort.* Please note that in another letter, she wrote just: *Dear Major de Châteaufort... I shall be doubly grateful to you*, there's no mistaking what that means. And look, here's a word scratched out, it's *all*, she wanted to put *all my regards* but didn't dare, and *all good wishes* wasn't strong enough, so she didn't finish her letter... Well, old man, I suppose you imagine that a well-brought-up young woman like Mme de Chaverny would throw herself into my arms like a little shop-girl...? I'm telling you that her letter is absolutely delightful and you must be blind not to see all the passion there is in it... And all those reproaches at the end, because I missed one of her Thursday at-homes, what do you say about that, eh?"

"Poor young woman!" exclaimed Perrin. "Don't lose your heart to him. You'll very quickly regret it!"

Châteaufort ignored his friend's outburst; but dropping his voice to an ingratiating whisper, he said:

"Do you know you could do me a great favour?"

"How?"

"By helping me in this affair. I know her husband treats her very badly – he's a beast who makes her very unhappy... You knew him yourself, didn't you? You must tell his wife that he's a brute, a man of the lowest possible reputation..."

"Good God!"

"A rake... you know he was. He had all sorts of mistresses when he was in the regiment... and what awful ones they were!... You must tell his wife all about it."

"But how on earth can one say that sort of thing... You know, between husband and wife..."

"Heavens above! There's a way of saying everything! Above all, say nice things about me."

"That's not so difficult, but..."

"It's not as easy as all that. Now listen, because if I let you say what you like, you'd go about it in a way that wouldn't suit my scheme at all. Tell her that you've *recently* noticed that I'm rather sad, that I don't talk, that I've lost my appetite…"

"No, really!" exclaimed Perrin with a huge laugh which made his pipe jump about in a most peculiar fashion. "I could never say that to Mme de Chaverny's face. Why, only last night, you nearly had to be carried out after that regimental dinner."

"All right, but there's no point in telling her that; but it is a good thing for her to know that I'm in love with her; and all those novelists have persuaded women that a man who's able to eat and drink can't be in love."

"Personally, I can't think of anything that would stop me from eating and drinking."

"Well, my dear Perrin," said Châteaufort, putting on his hat and arranging his curly hair, "that's all settled. I'll come and pick you up next Thursday: tails, silk stockings and pumps compulsory! Above all, don't forget to say awful things about the husband and lots of nice things about me."

He went out with an elegant flourish of his riding switch, leaving Major Perrin very perplexed about the invitation he had just received and even more worried at the thought of having to wear silk hose and evening dress.

4

THERE HAD BEEN a number of refusals and Mme de Chaverny's dinner party was a trifle dreary. Châteaufort was sitting next to Julie, assiduously attentive and as gay and charming as ever. As for Chaverny, he had been for a long ride that morning and was as hungry as a hunter: he ate and drank in a way that would make even a sick man ravenous. Major Perrin kept up with him, continually pouring out more drink and laughing uproariously at every ribald remark his host made. Chaverny, finding himself for once amongst soldiers, had immediately fallen back into the high spirits and lack of ceremony of the regimental mess; moreover, he had never been particularly noted for the refinement of his jokes. Each time he made some outrageous remark, his wife's face took on an icily disapproving expression and she would turn to Châteaufort and start a private conversation to avoid seeming to hear remarks which she found offensive.

Here is a sample of the refinement of this model husband. Towards the end of dinner, the talk having come round to the Opera, they were discussing the relative merits of different dancers and, among others, were speaking very highly of a certain Mlle ***. Thereupon Châteaufort outdid everyone else, above all in praise of her graceful figure and her modest manner.

Perrin, whom Châteaufort had taken to the Opera a few days before and who had only been on that one occasion, remembered Mlle *** very well.

"Wasn't she the girl," he enquired, "who leapt about like a gazelle? The one whose legs you kept on talking about, Châteaufort?"

"Aha! you were talking about her legs!" shouted Chaverny. "But do you know that if you talk too much about them, you're going to fall out with your C.O., the Duke of J***! So be warned, my friend!"

"But I don't suppose he's so jealous as to want to stop someone looking at them through opera glasses."

"On the contrary, he's as proud of them as if he'd discovered them himself. What do you think, Major Perrins?"

"The only legs I know anything about are horses' legs," replied the old soldier bashfully.

"It's quite true that they are superb," went on Chaverny, "and there isn't a nicer pair in Paris except..." He stopped and started twirling his moustache, giving a facetious look at his wife who at once coloured up to the eyes.

"Except those belonging to Mlle D***?" interrupted Châteaufort, mentioning the name of another dancer.

"No," replied Chaverny in a tragic Hamlet-like voice, "but do look at my wife."

Julie became scarlet with indignation and looked quickly and full of rage and contempt at her husband. Then, controlling herself with an effort, she turned sharply towards Châteaufort:

"We must study the duet from *Maometto* together," she said, her voice trembling slightly. "It's surely just right for your voice."

Chaverny was not easily put off.

"Did you know, Châteaufort," he went on, "that I tried to have a plaster cast made of those legs I mentioned? But she wouldn't consent."

Châteaufort, though highly delighted at this extremely tactless revelation, pretended not to have heard and went on talking to Mme de Chaverny about *Maometto*.

"The owner of them," continued the husband mercilessly, "used to be quite shocked when they received the admiration that they deserved but she wasn't really annoyed, in her heart of hearts. Did you know that she has her stockings made to measure specially by her own man – don't get angry Julie, I mean by her own woman, of course. And when I went to Brussels, I took three whole pages of most detailed instructions for the purchase of stockings."

But he was wasting his time, for Julie was determined not to hear a word. She went on chatting with Châteaufort, putting on a show of gaiety and trying to persuade him, by her gracious smiles, that she was listening only to him. Châteaufort, on the other hand, seemed completely immersed in *Maometto*; but he was not missing a single one of Chaverny's impertinent remarks.

After dinner there was music and Mme de Chaverny sang at the piano with Châteaufort. Chaverny disappeared the moment the piano was opened. A number of people arrived but this did not prevent Châteaufort from having long whispered conversations with Julie. When they left, he told Perrin that he hadn't wasted his time and that the affair was progressing nicely.

Perrin saw nothing wrong in a husband's talking about his wife's legs and when he was alone in the street with Châteaufort, he said to him, in a voice full of conviction:

"How can you have the heart to come between such a devoted couple! He's so fond of his little wife!"

5

FOR THE LAST MONTH, Chaverny had been much concerned with the idea of being appointed gentleman-in-waiting. You may perhaps be surprised that a fat, lazy man, liking his creature comforts, should not be proof against ambition; but he was full of good reasons to justify himself. First of all, he would say to his friends, I spend a lot of money on boxes at the theatre and opera to offer to women. When I have a post at court, I'll be able to have all the boxes I want, without paying a penny. And you know all that one can get by the offer of a box. In the next place, I'm very fond of shooting and all the royal shoots will be open to me. Lastly, now I've given up wearing uniform, I don't know what clothes to wear at my wife's dances. I'm not fond of dressing like a marquess; court dress will suit me very well. As a result, he was making discreet approaches. He would have liked his wife to do the same, too, but she had stubbornly refused, although she had a number of influential friends. Chaverny had done a couple of good turns to the Duke of H***, who was very powerful at court at that time, and he was relying a good deal on his support. His friend Châteaufort, also on good terms with the right people, was aiding and abetting him with that single-minded devotion that you may yourself be lucky enough to experience if you happen to have a pretty wife.

One incident greatly helped Chaverny's schemes, although it could have had rather disastrous consequences for him. Madame de Chaverny, not without some trouble, had managed to obtain a box at the Opera for a certain first night. This box held six people. Her husband, wonderful to relate, had agreed to go with her, though only under protest. In point of fact, Julie was anxious to offer Châteaufort a seat and feeling that she couldn't go to the Opera with him alone, she had bullied her husband into coming with them.

Immediately after the first act, Chaverny went off, leaving his wife alone with her friend. At first, there was a rather embarrassed silence, because Julie had for some time past felt embarrassed when she was alone with Châteaufort and the latter, in accordance with his little scheme, thought it appropriate to appear to be feeling emotional. Casting a surreptitious glance into the auditorium, he was delighted to see several of his acquaintances turning their opera-glasses towards the box. He was highly gratified at the thought that several of his friends would be feeling envious of his good luck and, to all appearances, were imagining it to be much greater than it really was.

Julie, having sniffed her scent bottle and her flowers several times, talked about the heat, the opera and the dresses. Châteaufort listened with only half an ear, gave a sigh or two, wriggled in his chair, looked at Julie and gave another sigh. Julie was beginning to feel rather ill at ease. All at once, he burst out:

"How I wish we were still living in the age of chivalry!"

"The age of chivalry? But why?" enquired Julie. "I suppose because you fancy yourself in medieval costume?"

"You must think I'm very conceited," he said bitterly, in a melancholy voice. "No, I should like it because in those days a man who was brave could aspire to all sorts of things... After all, the only thing you had to do to please your lady-love was to go and crack the skull of some giant... Look, can you see that big brute on the balcony? I wish you'd tell me to go and pull his ears so that afterwards I could have the right to whisper just three tiny words..."

"What a mad idea!" exclaimed Julie, blushing to the roots of her hair, for she guessed what those three tiny words were. "But just look at Mme de Sainte-Hermine in that low-necked dress at her age!"

"I can only see one thing and that is that you won't listen to me and I've seen it for a long time... Well, it's what you wish, so I'll keep quiet; but," he added very softly, with a sigh, "I hope you've understood my meaning."

33

"Indeed I haven't," retorted Julie, sharply. "But where on earth is my husband?"

An opportune caller came to save her further embarrassment. Châteaufort did not open his mouth. He had gone pale and seemed deeply moved. When the visitor left, he made one or two trivial references to the opera. There were long intervals of silence.

The second act was just starting when the box door opened and Chaverny appeared with a very pretty and lavishly dressed woman wearing magnificent pink plumes in her hair. He was followed by the Duke of H***.

"My dear," he said to his wife, "I found his Grace and this lady in an awful little box at the side where all you could see were the decorations. They were good enough to accept a seat in ours."

Julie bowed rather distantly: she didn't like the Duke of H***. The Duke and the pink befeathered lady were profuse in their apologies and hoped they weren't disturbing her. They prepared to sit down, with everyone politely offering everyone else the best seats. In the ensuing confusion, Châteaufort bent forwards and whispered very quickly into Julie's ear:

"Whatever you do, don't sit at the front."

Julie, quite amazed, remained seated where she was. When everyone had sat down, she turned to Châteaufort and rather sternly asked him for an explanation of the mystery. He was sitting with his head in the air, tight-lipped and his whole attitude showed that he was extremely upset. Julie misinterpreted his motives: she thought that he wanted to carry on a private conversation with her during the performance and continue his peculiar behaviour, which would have been impossible had she stayed in front. When she looked down at the auditorium again, she noticed that a number of women had their glasses turned towards the box; but this always happened whenever a new face appeared. People were whispering and smiling; but what was there extraordinary in that? Everybody is always so absurdly provincial at the Opera!

The unknown lady leant forwards to look at Julie's bouquet and said, with a charming smile:

"What lovely flowers you've got there! I'm sure they must have been very expensive at this time of year: at least ten francs. But I suppose you were given them, weren't you? Ladies never buy their own flowers."

Julie's eyes opened wide with astonishment and she tried to think who this woman could be; she supposed, someone from the depths of the country.

"Duke," said the lady in a melting voice, "you forgot to give me any flowers." Chaverny rushed to the door, the Duke tried to stop him and the lady, too; she didn't really want any flowers now. Julie exchanged a glance with Châteaufort. It said: "Thank you, but it's too late now." But she still hadn't guessed all.

During the whole performance, the befeathered lady tapped out the wrong beat with her fingers and talked utter nonsense about music. She submitted Julie to an interrogation on the price of her dress, her jewels and her horses. Julie who had never met such manners before, assumed that she must be some cousin of the Duke's who had just arrived from the depths of Brittany. When Chaverny came back with a bunch of flowers, far more splendid than his wife's, there was an endless succession of admiring comments, thanks and apologies.

"M. de Chaverny, I'm not ungrateful," said the supposed provincial. "To prove it, remind me to 'promise you something' as Shakespeare says. Yes, I'll embroider a purse for you when I've finished the one I've promised the duke."

At last the opera came to an end, to the great satisfaction of Julie who felt most uncomfortable beside her peculiar neighbour. The Duke offered her his arm and Chaverny took the other lady's. Châteaufort, very glum and irritable, brought up the rear, greeting very stiffly the acquaintances he met on the stairs.

Some ladies passed by close to them: Julie knew them by sight. A young man whispered something to them with a grin and they immediately stared with great curiosity at Chaverny and his wife and one of them exclaimed:

"It can't be true!"

The Duke's carriage came up: he took his leave of Mme de Chaverny, thanking her once again for all her kindness. However, Chaverny insisted on accompanying the lady to the duke's carriage and Julie and Châteaufort were left alone for a moment.

"Who on earth is that woman?" asked Julie.

"I mustn't say because it's quite fantastic!"

"What is?"

"Anyway, anyone who knows you will understand what it was all about... But Chaverny! I shouldn't have believed it."

"But what on earth is it all about? For goodness sake, do tell me. Who is that woman?"

Chaverny was on his way back. Châteaufort lowered his voice:

"The Duke's mistress, Mme Mélanie R***."

"Heavens above!" cried Julie looking at Châteaufort quite aghast. "It's not possible!"

Châteaufort shrugged his shoulders and taking her to her carriage, he added:

"That's exactly what those ladies were saying on the staircase. As for her, she's not so bad in her own way. She's really quite a stickler for the proprieties. She's even got a husband somewhere."

"My dear," announced Chaverny gleefully, "you don't need me to take you home, I know. Goodnight. I'm off to supper at the Duke's."

Julie did not reply.

"Châteaufort," went on Chaverny, "will you come with me to the Duke's? You're invited, they've just said so. You've made a good impression, you lucky dog."

Châteaufort rather coolly declined. He took his leave of Mme de Chaverny who sat chewing her handkerchief with rage as her carriage drew away.

"Now, old boy," said Chaverny, "at least you'll drop me at the Duke's in your gig."

"Delighted," replied Châteaufort very cheerfully, "but, by the way, I suppose you know that your wife finally realized whom she was sitting next to?"

"Impossible."

"Not at all. It was very wrong of you."

"Well, it can't be helped. She has extremely nice manners and besides, people don't know much about her yet. The Duke takes her about with him all the time."

6

Mme de Chaverny spent a very restless night. Her husband's behaviour at the Opera was the culmination of all his previous conduct and seemed to her to demand an immediate separation. Tomorrow, she would have it out with him and announce her intention of living not one minute longer under the same roof as a man who had compromised her so grievously. And yet she was scared at the thought of having it out with him. She had never had any sort of serious conversation with her husband and up till now she had always expressed her annoyance by sulking, which Chaverny always ignored. As he left his wife completely free in her actions, it would never have occurred to him to imagine that she might not want to allow him the liberties that he was prepared, if need be, to allow her. Above all, she was afraid of bursting into tears in the middle of the argument and then Chaverny might imagine that she was crying because she had been wounded in her love for him. She found herself bitterly regretting that her mother wasn't there, for she would have been able to advise her or even announce the separation herself. All these considerations put her into a state of great uncertainty and when she at last fell asleep, she had decided to go and consult one of her woman friends, who had known her when she was still quite young, and to rely on her shrewdness to advise her how to act towards Chaverny.

While she was giving rein to her indignation, she could not help making an involuntary comparison between her husband and Châteaufort. Her husband's monstrous breach of manners acted as a foil to the latter's tactfulness and she found it not unpleasant to reflect (although she blamed herself for doing so) that her lover was more anxious about her reputation than was her husband. This moral comparison led, in spite of herself, to a consideration of Châteaufort's elegance of manner and her husband's somewhat undistinguished appearance. She recalled her husband, with his rather big stomach, fussing round the Duke of H***'s mistress, while Châteaufort, more respectful than ever, seemed anxious to make up for all the respect her husband was probably causing her to lose. Finally, since our thoughts often carry us away in spite of ourselves, the thought crossed her mind more than once that if she by any chance were to become a widow, she would be young and rich and nothing would then stand in the way of giving Châteaufort's devotion its due reward. After all, one unsuccessful attempt was not conclusive proof against the institution of marriage and if Châteaufort's attachment were really sincere... But then she began to feel rather ashamed of her thoughts, so she banished them from her mind with the resolution to be more cautious than ever in her relations with him.

She woke up with a bad headache and still as far away as ever from taking any definite step. She decided not to go down to breakfast for fear of meeting her husband and so she had tea brought up to her room and ordered her carriage for her visit to Mme Lambert, the friend whom she wanted to consult and who was at the moment staying at her country house at P***.

While she was breakfasting, she opened the paper. The first thing she saw was this:

M. Darcy, First Secretary in the French Embassy in Constantinople arrived back in Paris with dispatches the day before yesterday. Immediately on his arrival, the young diplomatic officer called on the Minister of Foreign Affairs, with whom he had a long conference.

"Darcy in Paris!" she exclaimed. "I shall enjoy meeting him again. I wonder if he's become pompous. *The young diplomatic officer.* Fancy Darcy being a young diplomat!" And she couldn't help laughing to herself at the expression.

Darcy had been a very faithful visitor to Mme de Lussan's receptions, when he was attached to the Ministry of Foreign

Affairs in Paris. He had left Paris some time before Julie's marriage and she had not seen him since. She only knew that he had travelled about a great deal and had received rapid promotion.

She was still holding the paper in her hands when her husband came in. He seemed in great good humour. At the sight of him, she got up to go; but as she would have had to pass close by him to reach her dressing room, she remained standing where she was, so upset that the table shook under her hand, making all the breakfast service rattle.

"My dear," said Chaverny, "I've come to say goodbye for a few days. I'm going shooting at the Duke of H***'s place. I must tell you how delighted he was at your hospitality last night. My little scheme's going well and he's promised to put my name forward to the King."

As she listened, Julie's face was becoming alternately flushed and pale.

"Well, he owes you that at least," she said, her voice quivering. "He can hardly do less for someone who compromises his wife in such a disgusting way with his protector's mistresses."

Then, with a desperate effort, she stalked across the floor and went into her dressing room, banging the door.

For a moment, Chaverny looked sheepish.

"How the devil does she know that?" he thought. "But, anyway, what does it matter? What's done can't be undone!"

And as he was not in the habit of dwelling on unpleasant thoughts, he spun round, took a piece of sugar from the sugar bowl and, with his mouth full, exclaimed to the maid as she came in:

"Tell my wife I'll be at the Duke of H***'s for four or five days and I'll send her some game."

He went out with no further thought than for all the pheasant and deer he was going to slaughter.

7

W HEN JULIE LEFT FOR P***, she was even more angry with her husband, but this time for quite a trivial reason. For his trip to the Duke of H***'s castle, he had taken the new carriage, leaving his wife the old one which, according to the coachman, needed repairs.

During the journey, Mme de Chaverny set about preparing her story of the incident for Mme Lambert. In spite of her vexation, she was still not indifferent to the satisfaction which everyone feels at having a good story to tell and she set to work on it with particular attention to the beginning, trying first one gambit and then another. The result was that she was able to view her husband's outrageous behaviour from every aspect and her resentment grew in proportion.

As everyone knows, it is about fifteen miles from Paris to P*** and although Mme de Chaverny's speech for the prosecution was a long one, it will be quite obvious that, however venomous she felt, it was impossible to keep turning over the same idea in her mind for miles at a stretch. So, with that strange capacity that we have for associating pleasant with unpleasant things, gently nostalgic memories began to mingle with the violent feelings aroused by her husband's misdemeanours.

The clear sharp air, the bright sun and the cheerful faces of the passers-by helped to distract her from her bad temper. She recalled scenes from her childhood, days when she used to go on country walks with young people of her own age. She went back once more to her convent and her companions there, joined in their games and took part in the meals. At last she was able to understand those mysterious secrets which she had overheard the big girls confiding to each other and she could not help smiling as she thought of the hundred little ways in which women betray, even from an early age, their instinctive interest in men.

Next her memories turned to her coming-out. She went over all the most brilliant balls she had been to in the year immediately following her departure from the convent. She had forgotten all the others: how quickly one becomes *blasé*! But these balls reminded her of her husband. "I must have been mad," she said to herself, "how was it that I didn't realize from the start that I couldn't ever be happy with him?" Every solecism, every platitude which poor Chaverny, in common with all prospective husbands, had brought out with such aplomb during the month before her marriage, was carefully noted down in her memory. At the same time, she could not help thinking of all the numerous admirers who had been so bitterly disappointed when she married and who had themselves married all the same (or found other consolations) a month or two later. "Should I have been happy with anyone else?" she asked herself. "A*** was certainly very stupid, but at least he's inoffensive and his wife does just as she likes with him. You can always manage to get on with a husband who does what he's told. B*** goes about with other women and his wife is sentimental enough to take it to heart. All the same, he's extremely considerate and… that would suit me well enough. Then there's young Count C*** who's always busy reading some pamphlet or other so that he can become a Deputy, I suppose he'll make a good husband one day… Yes, but they are all boring and ugly and stupid…" As she went over the list of all the young men she had known before her marriage, for the second time Darcy's name came to mind.

In the old days, Darcy had been a person of no consequence whatsoever in Mme de Lussan's set, because it was known – certainly every mother knew – that his lack of money would never permit him to think of marrying any of their daughters. And as far as the daughters themselves were concerned, there was nothing about him to turn their pretty young heads. In other respects, he had the reputation of being a gentleman. Being something of a misanthrope as well as having rather a caustic tongue, he enjoyed making fun of the absurdities and pretensions of the other young men, whenever he found himself the only man in a group of girls. When he was seen whispering to some girl, their mamas were not alarmed, because their daughters used to laugh out loud and mothers with daughters who had nice teeth even used to say that M. Darcy was an extremely pleasant young man.

A similarity of tastes and a mutual respect for each other's capacity for tittle-tattle had brought Julie and Darcy together. After a skirmish or two, they had made a pact of non-aggression, an offensive and defensive alliance: they kept their hands off each other but were always ready to join forces to give their friends the benefit of their... kind nature.

One evening, Julie had been asked to sing. She had a good voice and she knew it. As she went to the piano, she looked at the other women rather arrogantly before starting to sing, almost as if challenging them. But that evening, either because she was indisposed or perhaps because of some malignant fate, her voice cracked. The first note from her normally tuneful voice was almost a croak. Julie lost her head, sang all the wrong notes and muffed all the trills: in short, she made a complete fiasco. Completely flustered and almost in tears, poor Julie left the piano and as she went back to her place, she could not help noticing the malicious pleasure of her friends at witnessing her humiliation. Even the men seemed to be smiling to themselves rather unkindly. She dropped her eyes in shame and anger and did not dare to raise them for some time. When she finally did so, the first friendly face she saw was Darcy's. He had gone quite pale and there were tears in his eyes; he seemed more affected by her mishap than she was. "He's in love with me!" she thought, "he's really in love with me." That night she hardly slept and Darcy's sad face haunted her all the time. For two days, she thought only of him and the secret passion which he must feel for her. The romance was already forming in her mind when one day Mme de Lussan found that Darcy had left his card on her, to announce his departure.

"Where's M. Darcy going?" Julie asked one of his friends.

"Where's he going? Why, didn't you know? He's going to Constantinople. He's leaving tonight with the diplomatic bag."

"So he doesn't love me!" she thought. A week later, Darcy had been forgotten; but he, for his part, being still rather romantic at that time, took eight months to forget her. To be fair to her, one can explain this considerable difference in the length of their memories by remembering that Darcy was surrounded by barbarians, whereas Julie, in Paris, was surrounded by all sorts of admirers and amusements.

However this may be, six or seven years after they had parted, Julie in her carriage taking her to P*** still had not forgotten Darcy's dismal expression the day she sang so badly; and it must be confessed that she thought how he had probably loved her at that time and perhaps she even thought how he might still feel towards her. All this interested her quite considerably for a couple of miles. Then Darcy was finally forgotten for the third time.

8

JULIE WAS NOT A LITTLE PUT OUT when she saw, as she drove into P***, that there was a carriage being unhitched in Mme Lambert's drive, a sure sign of a visitor intending to make a long call. Consequently it would not be possible to embark on her tale of woe concerning M. de Chaverny.

When Julie was shown into the drawing room, Mme Lambert was with a woman whom Julie had met before but whom she knew only by name. She had difficulty in hiding her annoyance at having wasted her trip to P***.

"Good evening, my dear!" exclaimed Mme Lambert, kissing her. "How nice to see you haven't quite forgotten me! You couldn't have come at a better time, because we're expecting a crowd of people who will all be terribly glad to see you."

Julie replied wanly that she had been hoping to find Mme Lambert alone.

"They'll be absolutely delighted to see you," went on Mme Lambert. "My house has been so dreary since my daughter was married that I'm only too pleased when all my kind friends come and meet here. But my dear child, what have you done with your rosy cheeks? You look quite pale today." Julie concocted an explanation: the long journey… the dust… the heat…

"As it happens, I've two of your admirers coming to dinner this evening, who will be having a nice surprise – M. de Châteaufort and probably his faithful shadow, Major Perrin."

"I had the pleasure of entertaining Major Perrin recently," said Julie, blushing a little, for she was thinking of Châteaufort.

"I've also got M. de St Léger. He really must organize some charades here one evening next month and you must come and join in, my dear. You were our first string for charades, two years ago."

"My goodness, it's so long since I played them, I'm sure I would never recover the confidence I used to have."

"Ah, Julie my child, guess who's coming as well. But you'll have to use your memory, my dear, to remember *his* name."

Darcy's name immediately sprang into Julie's mind.

"I've got him on the brain," she thought. "My memory, Mme Lambert?" she went on. "I've a good memory."

"I mean one that can go back about six or seven years… Do you remember one of your beaux when you were a little girl and wore your hair in ribbons?"

"I really can't guess."

"How awful you are, my dear! Forgetting a charming young man whom you used to like a great deal, unless I'm very much mistaken; so much so, that your mama was a little bit alarmed by it. Well now, my sweet, since you forget your old flames like this I'll have to refresh your memory: it's M. Darcy."

"M. Darcy?"

"Yes. He's back from Constantinople at last, only a couple of days ago. He came to see me the day before yesterday and I invited him here. And do you know, you ungrateful young woman, that he was so eager to ask after you that I was most suspicious!"

"M. Darcy?" said Julie hesitantly, pretending not to remember. "M. Darcy? Wasn't he a tall fair young man? A secretary in some embassy?"

"My dear, you won't recognize him. He's changed a lot. He's pale or sallow, rather, with deep-set eyes. He's lost a lot of hair, because of the heat, at least that's what he says. In two or three years time, if he goes on like that, he'll be quite bald in front, although he's not quite thirty yet."

At this point the lady, who was listening to Darcy's misfortune, interrupted to recommend most warmly the use of Kalydor, which had apparently done wonders for her when her hair had started dropping out after an illness. She took care, while saying this, to run her hand through her thick heavy curls of beautiful light brown hair.

"Has Darcy been in Constantinople all the time?" asked Mme de Chaverny.

"Not quite, because he's travelled about quite a bit. He's been into Russia and all over Greece. Hadn't you heard what luck he's just had? His uncle has died and left him a lot of money. He also went to Asia Minor, to... where was it he said? – to Caramanio. He's absolutely charming, my dear, and full of the most wonderful stories which will quite entrance you. Yesterday he told me so many amusing things that I kept on saying to him: 'You must keep them until tomorrow. You'll be able to tell them to the ladies instead of wasting them on an old woman like me.'"

"Did he tell you his story about the Turkish woman he rescued?" asked Mme Dumanoir, the advocate of Kalydor.

"The Turkish woman he rescued? Did he rescue a Turkish woman? He didn't say a word about it to me."

"Really? But it was a tremendous feat, straight out of a novel!"

"Oh, please tell us about it!"

"No, you must ask him yourself. I've only heard the story from my sister, whose husband, as you know, was consul in Smyrna. But she had it from an Englishman who was actually present at the whole thing. It's a marvellous story."

"Do tell us, Mme Dumanoir. How can you possibly expect us to wait till dinner? There's nothing so miserable as hearing all about a story that you don't know."

"Well, I'm sure I'll spoil it, but anyway, this is what I was told: M. Darcy was in Turkey examining some sort of ruins beside the sea when he saw a very gloomy procession approaching. It was some people carrying a sack and this sack could be seen moving about as if there was something alive inside."

"Oh my goodness!" exclaimed Mme Lambert, who knew her Byron, "it was a woman who was going to be thrown into the sea!"

"Exactly," went on Mme Dumanoir, rather nettled at being thus deprived of the most dramatic incident of her story.

"M. Darcy looked at the sack, heard a low moan and at once guessed the horrid truth. He asked the men what they were doing but their only reply was to draw their daggers. Fortunately M. Darcy was well armed and chased them away. Then out of the horrible sack, he pulled a woman, half unconscious and ravishingly lovely. He took her back to the town and put her in a place of safety."

"Poor woman!" said Julie, beginning to become interested in the story.

"But do you think she was safe? Not a bit of it. The jealous husband – it was a husband, of course – stirred up the local inhabitants and they went round to M. Darcy's house to burn him alive. I'm not quite certain how the affair ended. All that I do know is that he was besieged and finally succeeded in getting the woman to a safe place. They even say," she added with a sudden change of tone, like a priest intoning the responses, "that M. Darcy took the trouble to have her converted and baptised."

"And did he marry her as well?" asked Julie smiling.

"That I don't know. But the Turkish woman... she had a most peculiar name, she was called Eminy... she fell madly in love with Darcy. My sister said that all the time she called him: *Sotir, Sotir* – that means 'My saviour' in Turkish or Greek. Eulalie told me she was one of the most beautiful persons you would ever meet."

"We'll pull his leg about his Turk!" exclaimed Mme Lambert. "Shan't we, ladies? We must tease him a bit... Actually, this action of Darcy's doesn't surprise me in the least. He's one of the most generous persons in the world and I know certain things that he's done which bring tears to my eyes every time I think of them. His uncle died leaving an illegitimate daughter whom he'd never acknowledged. As he didn't leave a will and she had no rights on his estate, Darcy, who was the only legatee, insisted on her having a share and a share that was probably much larger than his uncle would have left her."

"Is she pretty, the illegitimate daughter?" asked Julie, rather nastily, because she was beginning to feel an urge to say something unkind about this M. Darcy whom she couldn't succeed in forgetting.

"But my dear, how could you think such a thing? But anyway, Darcy was still in Constantinople when his uncle died and probably never saw the daughter."

The arrival of Châteaufort, Major Perrin and a few other guests put an end to the conversation. Châteaufort sat down beside Mme de Chaverny and took advantage of a moment when everyone was talking very loudly to say to her:

"You look sad. I should be very sorry if anything I said to you yesterday was the cause of it?"

Mme de Chaverny didn't hear what he said, or rather did not want to hear. Châteaufort had thus to suffer the mortification of having to repeat what he had said and the still greater mortification of receiving a rather tart retort, after which Julie at once joined in the general conversation and, changing her seat, left the unhappy swain sitting by himself.

Nothing daunted, Châteaufort started making funny remarks, without much success. Mme de Chaverny, who was the only person he wished to impress, was listening with only half an ear. She was thinking that Darcy would soon be there, at the same time wondering why she was worrying so much about a man whom she ought to have forgotten and who in any case had probably long since forgotten her.

At last the sound of a carriage was heard; the drawing-room door opened.

"Ah, there he is!" exclaimed Mme Lambert.

Julie did not dare turn her head but went extremely pale and suddenly felt cold all over. It was all she could do to recover sufficiently to prevent Châteaufort from noticing the change in her face.

Darcy kissed Mme Lambert's hand and stood talking to her for a moment before sitting down beside her. A long pause ensued: Mme Lambert seemed to be hoping for some recognition and trying to lead up to it. Châteaufort and all the other men, with the exception of the worthy Major Perrin, were all eyeing Darcy with curiosity not unmixed with jealousy. Fresh as he was from Constantinople, he had a great advantage over them and this was enough to make them adopt an attitude of stiffness and formality such as one usually reserves for strangers. Darcy, who had paid no attention to anyone, was the first to break the silence. He talked about the weather, his journey, the first thing that came into his head. His voice was soft and musical. Mme de Chaverny risked a glance towards him: she saw him in profile. He seemed to be thinner and his expression was different... On the whole, she approved.

"My dear Darcy," said Mme Lambert, "take a good look around you and see if you can't find an old friend of yours."

Darcy turned his head and suddenly saw Julie who had been hiding behind the brim of her hat. He jumped up with an exclamation of surprise and went over to her, hand outstretched; then, stopping short as if regretting his over-familiarity, he bowed very low to Julie and, with proper formality, told her how very pleased he was to see her again. Julie stammered a polite phrase or two and blushed deeply when she saw that Darcy was still standing over her and eyeing her closely.

She soon regained her composure and then, in her turn, gave him that look, both vague and searching, which the well-bred use when necessary. He was a tall, pale young man, with a calm expression which seemed to spring less from his nature than from the practice of self-control. His forehead was already deeply furrowed. His eyes were deep-set, the corners of his mouth turned down and his temples were beginning to recede, although he could not have been over thirty. He was dressed very simply but with the elegance which comes from frequenting good society and a casualness that contrasted with the affectation of many young men. Julie took all these things in with pleasure. She observed, too, on his forehead a longish scar, rather like a sabre wound, which was only half hidden by a lock of hair.

Julie was sitting beside Mme Lambert. Between her and Châteaufort there was a chair, but as soon as Darcy had stood up, Châteaufort put his hand on the back of it and tipped it up on one of its legs, obviously playing the part of dog in the manger. Mme Lambert, however, took pity on Darcy, who was still on his feet in front of Julie and made room for him beside her on the settee on which she was sitting. Darcy thus found himself next to Julie. He quickly made the most of this advantage and launched on a long conversation with her.

However, he still had to submit to a long cross-examination from Mme Lambert and one or two others as to his travels, but got out of it as briefly as he could and lost no opportunity of returning to his private conversation with Mme de Chaverny.

"Give Mme de Chaverny your arm," said Mme Lambert to Darcy as the bell rang for dinner. Châteaufort bit his lips but managed to find a place close to Julie in order to keep his eye on her at table.

9

Aafter dinner, as it was a lovely evening and the weather warm, the guests took their coffee round a rustic table in the garden.

Châteaufort had been observing with growing resentment the attention Darcy was showing Mme de Chaverny and as he saw, too, the interest she seemed to be taking in the newcomer's conversation, he became more and more disagreeable so that the only effect of his jealousy was to make him less likeable himself. He paced up and down on the terrace where the guests were sitting, unable to keep still, like most people who are upset, now and then looking up at the large black clouds forming on the horizon but more often watching his rival chatting in a low voice with Julie. Sometimes he saw her smile and then become serious; at others, she shyly dropped her eyes. In fact, he could see plainly that every word that Darcy spoke had considerable effect on her; but what irritated him most was that all the varied expressions on Julie's face were merely the echo or reflection of Darcy's own expressive features. At last, able to stand his torment no longer, he walked up to her and bending over the back of her chair at a moment when Darcy was giving someone information about the Sultan's beard, he said bitterly:

"M. Darcy seems to be a most pleasant person."

"Yes, indeed!" replied Mme de Chaverny, unable to hide her enthusiasm.

"He must be so," went on Châteaufort, "to make you forget your old friends."

"My old friends," said Julie in a rather sarcastic tone. "I don't know what you mean." And she turned her back on him. Then, taking hold of a corner of the handkerchief in Mme Lambert's hand: "What charming embroidery!" she said. "It's wonderfully done."

"Do you think so, my dear? It's a present from M. Darcy who has brought me I don't know how many embroidered handkerchiefs back from Constantinople. By the way, Darcy, was it your Turkish woman who embroidered them?"

"My Turkish woman? What Turkish woman?"

"You know, that beautiful Sultan's wife whose life you saved and who used to call you... oh yes, we know all about it... who used to call you... oh, her saviour, anyway. You must know the Turkish for that."

Darcy laughed and clapped his hand to his forehead.

"It can't be possible," he exclaimed, "that the story of that unfortunate incident has already reached Paris!"

"But there's nothing unfortunate about it, except perhaps for the Panjandrum who lost his favourite wife."

"I'm afraid," replied Darcy, "that you only know half the story, for it was as wretched for me as the windmills were for Don Quixote. It can't really be possible that after causing so much amusement to my compatriots in Turkey, I'm going to have my leg pulled in Paris for the only piece of knight-errantry I've ever indulged in?"

"What's all this? But we haven't heard anything about it! Do tell us about it!" cried all the ladies in chorus.

"I ought really to leave you with the version that you already know," said Darcy, "and not tell you the sequel, because it brings back memories that are not very pleasant; but one of my friends, Sir John Tyrrel is shortly coming to Paris – I must ask your permission to introduce him to you, Mme Lambert – and he also played a part in this tragi-comedy and he might quite well think it funny to make me look even more absurd than I really was. So here are the facts: once the poor woman was installed in the French consulate…"

"Oh, but you must begin at the beginning!" cried Mme Lambert.

"But you already know it."

"No, we don't know anything and we insist on your telling the story from beginning to end."

"Very well then. First I must explain that in 18** I was in

Larnaca and one day I went out sketching in the country. I had a very agreeable young Englishman with me, a very good sort and a very good trencherman, too, called Sir John Tyrrel. He was a most useful travelling companion because he's always thinking about food and he never forgot to bring enough to eat. Also, he was always cheerful. What is more, he was travelling without any particular aim and he knew absolutely nothing about botany or geology, which are both very tiresome things in travelling companions.

"I was sitting in the shade of a tumble-down old house, about a couple of hundred yards away from cliffs which, at that particular spot, fell sheer into the sea. I was busy sketching the remains of an ancient sarcophagus while Sir John, lying in the grass, was poking fun at my unfortunate passion for the fine arts and smoking delicious Latakian tobacco. Nearby, a Turkish dragoman, whom we had engaged as a servant, was busy making some coffee. He was the best coffee-maker and the biggest coward of any Turk I've ever known.

"All of a sudden, Sir John shouted out joyfully: 'Here come some people from the hills with some snow. We'll buy some and make some orange sherbet.'

"I looked up and saw a donkey approaching with a big bundle slung over its back. Two slaves were supporting each end. In front, the donkey-boy was leading his donkey and a venerable white-bearded Turk brought up the rear on quite a decent horse. The whole procession was approaching very slowly and solemnly.

"Our Turk, busy puffing at his fire, glanced sideways at the laden donkey and said with a peculiar smile: 'It's not snow.' Then he went on making our coffee with his usual inscrutable calm.

"'What is it, then?' asked Tyrrel. 'Is it something to eat?'

"'Something for the fish to eat,' replied the Turk.

"At that moment the man on horseback galloped off towards the sea and passed close by us, not without one of those disdainful glances that Muslims are always giving Christians. He urged his horse to the edge of the cliffs and reined in at the steepest part. He stood looking down at the sea and seemed to be trying to find the most suitable place to jump down.

"We now looked more closely at the bundle on the donkey and were struck by the strange shape of the sack. All the stories about women drowned by jealous husbands suddenly came to our minds and we mentioned this thought to each other.

"'Ask those rascals,' said Sir John to our Turk, 'if that's not a woman they're carrying.'

"The Turk looked scared and opened his eyes very wide but not his mouth. It was plain that he thought our question much too indiscreet.

"At that moment, the sack was level with us and we could

distinctly see it moving about and even heard a sort of grunt or groan coming from it.

"Although Tyrrel's rather too fond of his stomach, he's also an extremely chivalrous person. He jumped up like a madman, ran up to the donkey-boy and asked him, in English because he was so beside himself with rage, what he was carrying and what he was going to do with the sack. The boy took good care not to answer, but the sack gave a jerk and we heard a woman's voice shouting. At this, the two slaves started slashing away at the sack with the straps they used to beat the donkey. Tyrrel completely lost his temper. With a well-aimed punch, he knocked the donkey-boy flat and seized one of the slaves by the throat, whereupon the sack tipped off with a bump on to the grass.

"I ran up too. The other slave was busy picking up stones and the donkey-boy getting to his feet. In spite of my dislike of interfering in other people's business, I couldn't possibly leave my companion in the lurch. I'd picked up a stick which I used to support my sunshade while sketching and I now waved it threateningly at the slaves and the donkey-boy with my most warlike look. Everything was going all right when that beggar of a Turk on his horse, having finished surveying the sea, turned round on hearing the noise. He came up like lightning and was on us before we had time to think. He had a nasty-looking sort of sword in his hand…"

"A yataghan?" said Châteaufort, who had a weakness for local colour.

"A yataghan," repeated Darcy with an approving smile. "He came right up to me and struck me a blow on the head with his yataghan which made me see... celestial bodies, as my friend the Marquess of Roseville used to say so elegantly. I retorted by giving him a smart blow on his back with my stick and then, even more enraged than my friend Tyrrel, I started swinging it round and round as hard as I could, hitting the donkey-boy, the slaves, the horse and the Turk. No doubt we should have come off badly because our dragoman was observing strict neutrality and we could hardly have defended our-selves for long with one stick against three infantrymen, one cavalry-man and a yataghan. Fortunately, Sir John remembered that we had brought a brace of pistols along with us. He got them out, threw one to me and quickly pointed the other one at the horseman who was causing all the trouble. The sight of the pistols and the click as they were cocked produced a magical effect on our opponents who retreated ignominiously, leaving us in possession of the field of battle, a sack and even a donkey. In spite of our rage, we didn't fire, which was a good thing, because you can't get away with killing a Muslim and it's quite expensive just to give one a good hiding.

"When I'd wiped away some of the blood, our first thought, as you can well imagine, was to go and open the sack. In it we found a woman, quite good-looking, though a trifle fat, with lovely black hair and wearing nothing but a long blue woollen chemise rather less transparent than Mme de Chaverny's scarf.

"She climbed quickly out of the sack and, without seeming particularly embarrassed, launched into a speech which was no doubt extremely moving but of which we didn't understand a single word. After which, she kissed my hand – the only time a lady has ever done me that honour.

"Meanwhile, we had calmed down. We saw that our dragoman was pulling his beard out in despair. I patched up my head as well as I could with my handkerchief. Tyrrel kept on saying:

"'What on earth can we do with the woman? If we stay here, the husband will certainly come back with reinforcements and make mincemeat of us. If we go back with the woman to Larnaca in the state we're in, the mob will certainly stone us to death.'

"And, quite nonplussed by all these thoughts, he exclaimed, having recovered his British phlegm:

"'What on earth possessed you to go sketching today?'

"His exclamation made me laugh and the woman, who hadn't understood a word, started to laugh too.

"But we had to take a decision. I thought that the best thing for us to do was to put ourselves under the protection of the

French consul; but the trouble was to find our way back to Larnaca. Dusk was falling and it was a lucky thing for us. Our Turk took us by a devious path and thanks to this and to the dark, we eventually arrived safely at the consul's house, which was outside the town. I forgot to say that we had meantime rigged the woman out, almost decently, in the sack and our dragoman's turban.

"The consul gave us a very frigid reception, told us we were out of our minds, that we should respect the habits and customs of the countries in which we were living and shouldn't interfere between husband and wife… In short, he told us off in no uncertain terms; and he was quite right because we could easily have caused a riot and got all the Europeans in Cyprus massacred.

"His wife was softer-hearted; she was a great novel-reader and thought our behaviour was very heroic. Indeed, we had behaved just like heroes in a novel. This excellent lady was also very religious; she thought she could easily convert the infidel we had brought her, that the conversion would appear in the papers and that her husband would be made a consul-general. The whole scheme came to her in a flash. She clasped the Turkish woman to her bosom, gave her a dress, made the consul ashamed of his heartlessness and sent him off to the Pasha to arrange the whole affair.

"The Pasha was beside himself with rage. The jealous

husband turned out to be a man of some importance and was out for blood. It was disgraceful, he declared, for dogs of Christians to prevent a man like himself from throwing his property into the sea. The consul was extremely embarrassed; he talked a lot about the King his master and still more about a sixty-gun frigate which had just appeared outside Larnaca. But the argument which produced the greatest effect was the suggestion that he made, in our name, to buy the slave at a fair price.

"Dear me, if you only knew what a Turk means by a fair price. We had to pay the husband, the Pasha, the donkey-boy who had had two teeth broken by Tyrrel, to pay for the fuss, in fact, to pay for everything. How often Tyrrel exclaimed mournfully:

"'Why on earth do people go sketching by the sea!'"

"What an adventure, you poor man!" cried Mme Lambert. "So that's how you got that terrible scar? Please, do lift up your hair. But it's a miracle he didn't cut your head right off!"

During the whole story, Julie had not once taken her eyes off Darcy's forehead; now she asked diffidently:

"What became of the woman?"

"That's just the part of the story I don't really like telling, because the sequel was so disconcerting for me that everybody's still laughing at me for our gallant exploit."

"Was she pretty, the woman?" asked Mme de Chaverny, blushing slightly.

"What was her name?" enquired Mme Lambert.

"Her name was Emineh."

"Pretty?"

"Yes, quite pretty, but too fat and too heavily made-up, following the custom of her country. You need a lot of practice to appreciate the charms of a Turkish beauty. Anyway, Emineh was installed in the consul's house. She was a Mingrelian and told the consul's wife that she was the daughter of a prince. In that country, any rogue who rules over ten other rogues is a prince. So she was treated like a princess. She dined at table and used to eat enough for three people. Then, whenever they tried to talk religion, she would regularly drop off to sleep. This went on for some time. Eventually, a day was fixed for the baptism. Mme C. appointed herself godmother and insisted on my being the godfather. This meant sweets, presents and all the rest! Mme C. used to say that Emineh liked me better than Tyrrel because whenever she passed me my coffee, she always spilt some on my clothes. I was getting ready for the baptism with a really evangelical piety when the day before the ceremony, the lovely Emineh disappeared. Must I tell you the whole story? The consul had a chef who was a Mingrelian, a rascal if ever there was one, but he cooked a magnificent pilaff. The Mingrelian had taken Emineh's fancy – I suppose she was patriotic in a peculiar sort of way. He ran off with her and with a fairly considerable sum of money at the same time, and it was never recovered. So the consul lost his money, his wife the trousseau she had given Emineh, I the gloves and sweets – not counting all the knocks I'd received. Worst of all, I was somehow made responsible for the whole affair. They all maintained it was I who had rescued the miserable woman whereas I really wished her at the bottom of the sea, particularly as she brought such bad luck to my friends. Tyrrel managed to extricate himself and was looked on as the victim whereas he was really the chief culprit in the fight and I was left with the reputation of being quixotic, as well as this scar which seriously hampers my success with women!"

After the end of the story, they went back into the drawing-room. Darcy chatted for a short while longer with Mme de Chaverny and then had to leave her to meet a young man who was deeply interested in political economy and, in preparation for a career in Parliament, wanted some statistical information about the Ottoman Empire.

10

A FTER DARCY LEFT HER, Julie kept looking at the clock. She was listening absent-mindedly to Châteaufort and in spite of herself, her eyes continually strayed to Darcy chatting at the other end of the room. Now and again he looked at her while talking to his lover of statistics and she found it difficult to face his searching gaze, placid though it was. She realized that he had already acquired an extraordinary power over her; and she no longer wanted to resist.

Finally, she asked for her carriage and either by accident or design, she looked at Darcy while asking for it, in a way which seemed to say: "You've wasted half an hour which we could have spent together." The carriage was announced. Darcy was still conversing but he seemed tired and bored by his questioner who would not let him go. Julie slowly stood up, shook hands with Mme Lambert and then went towards the drawing-room door, surprised and almost offended to see Darcy still remaining where he was. Châteaufort went with her and offered his arm which she took mechanically without hearing what he was saying and almost without noticing his presence.

She went across the hall with Mme Lambert and a few
other people who accompanied her as far as her carriage.
Darcy stayed in the drawing-room. Once she was seated,
Châteaufort asked her with a smile whether she would not
be afraid all alone on the road in the dark and added that he
was going to follow close behind in his own carriage as soon
as Major Perrin had finished his game of billiards. Julie, who
was day-dreaming, was brought back to reality by the sound
of his voice, but she had not understood a word. She did what
any other woman would have done in the circumstances: she
smiled at him. Then she nodded goodbye to the people on the
steps of the house and drove off at a good speed. However, just
as the carriage was moving off, she saw Darcy come out of the
drawing-room, looking pale and unhappy, his eyes fastened
on her as if begging a special parting greeting for himself.
She went off, sorry not to have been able to give him a nod
for himself alone and even thinking that he might be hurt
because of it. She had already quite forgotten that he had left
it to someone else to take her to her carriage; the fault seemed
entirely on her side and she blamed herself almost as if she
had committed some serious crime. Her feelings for Darcy
years ago, after the party when she had sung out of tune, were
much less strong than those she had now; not only had the
years strengthened her impressions, but they were reinforced
by all her accumulated anger for her husband. Perhaps even

the way she had been drawn towards Châteaufort (who, incidentally, was now relegated to oblivion) had made her the more ready to give way, without too many qualms, to her much stronger feelings for Darcy.

As for the latter, his thoughts were much less tumultuous. He had enjoyed meeting a pretty woman who recalled pleasant memories and whom he looked forward to meeting during the winter he was going to spend in Paris. But once she was out of sight, all that was left was, at most, the memory of a couple of amusing hours and even that memory was rather spoilt by the prospect of being late to bed and having to drive fifteen miles beforehand. We leave him then, absorbed in such prosaic reflections and muffling himself up carefully in his coat before settling down comfortably in his hired coupé, his thoughts wandering from Mme Lambert's drawing room to Constantinople, from Constantinople to Corfu and from Corfu into a gentle doze.

11

W HEN MME DE CHAVERNY left Mme de Lambert's house, the evening was horribly dark and sultry; now and then flashes of lightning lit up the landscape, making a black silhouette of trees against the livid orange background. After each flash, the darkness seemed doubly great and the coachman could not see his horses' heads. Soon, a violent storm broke. At first only falling in a few large drops, the rain quickly became a torrential flood. The sky was aflame on all sides and the heavenly cannonade was deafening. The frightened horses were snorting and rearing instead of moving forwards, but the coachman was fortified by a good supper; his thick hooded cape and, above all, the wine he had been drinking, prevented him from being afraid either of the water or the bad roads. He was furiously whipping up the poor beasts with all the intrepidity of Caesar when, during the storm, he exclaimed to his pilot: "You are carrying Caesar and his fate!"

Mme de Chaverny, not being afraid of thunder, hardly paid any attention to the storm. She was going over with herself all that Darcy had said to her and regretting that she had not said many of the things that she had wanted to, when she was suddenly interrupted in her musings by a violent jolt of her carriage while, at the same time, the windows were smashed to pieces and something snapped with an ominous sound. The carriage had been hurled into the ditch. Julie was unharmed, apart from the fright, but the rain was pelting down, a wheel was broken, the lamps had gone out and there was not a single house to take shelter. The coachman was swearing and the groom was cursing the coachman for his clumsiness. Julie stayed in her carriage and asked how it would be possible to get back to P*** or what was to be done, but, to all her questions, she received the same discouraging reply: "It can't be done."

However, the rumble of an approaching carriage was heard in the distance and soon Mme de Chaverny's coachman discerned, to his great satisfaction, one of his colleagues with whom he had laid the foundation of a close friendship in Mme Lambert's kitchen. He shouted to him to stop.

The carriage halted and hardly had Mme de Chaverny's name been mentioned than the young man in the coupé opened the door himself and crying out: "Is she hurt?" he leapt down beside Julie's carriage. She had recognized Darcy and she was waiting.

Their hands met in the darkness and Darcy thought he felt Mme de Chaverny's squeezing his; but it was probably because of the fright. After the first question or two, Darcy naturally offered her his carriage. For a moment, Julie hesitated, for she was not at all certain what she ought to do. On the one hand, if she wanted to reach Paris, she was thinking of the ten or twelve miles which still lay ahead, all alone with a young man; on the other, if she were to go back and throw herself on Mme Lambert's hospitality, she shuddered at the prospect of having to recount the romantic incident of the overturning of the carriage and of Darcy's help. Reappearing in the drawing room in the middle of a game of whist after having been rescued by Darcy, just like that Turkish woman... no, she couldn't possibly think of it! But there were also the ten long miles to Paris!... While she was thus hesitating and rather awkwardly stammering a few polite phrases about all the trouble she would be giving, Darcy, as if reading her inmost thoughts, said to her coldly: "Take my carriage, Mme de Chaverny. I'll wait in yours until someone comes by going to Paris."

Julie, afraid of appearing too prudish, hastily accepted his first suggestion but not the second and as she decided so rapidly, she had no time to settle the important question as to whether to go to P*** or to Paris. But before she was able to say where she wanted to go, she found herself ensconced in Darcy's carriage, wrapped in his cloak which he hastened to give her and the horses were trotting briskly towards Paris.

Her servant had taken the decision for her by giving the coachman his mistress's address.

Conversation was at first rather embarrassed on both sides. Darcy's manner was rather curt and he seemed somewhat annoyed. Julie supposed that he had been hurt by her hesitation and thought her ridiculously strait-laced; and she by now was so much under his influence that she took all the blame for it on to herself and wanted to mollify his bad humour, for which she felt responsible. She noticed that Darcy's coat was damp and taking off her own cloak, she insisted that he put it on. After protest, the discussion was settled by compromise and they finished by sharing the cloak – an imprudent move which she would never have made if she had not wanted to make him forget her original hesitation.

They were now so close that Julie could feel the heat of Darcy's breath on her cheek and the jolting of the carriage kept on bringing them even closer.

"Sharing this cloak," said Darcy, "reminds me of the charades we used to have. Do you remember being my Virginia when we dressed up in your grandmother's cape?"

"Yes, and I remember the telling-off she gave me, too."

"Ah, yes," said Darcy, "those were happy days. How often I've thought of those nice evenings at the rue de Bellechasse, sometimes with pleasure, sometimes unhappily. Do you remember those lovely vulture's wings which they tied on your shoulders with pink ribbon and the most artistic beak I made for you out of gold paper?"

"Yes," replied Julie, "you were Prometheus and I was the vulture. But what an extraordinary memory you've got. How can you possibly remember all those silly things? After all, it's such a long time since we met."

"Are you fishing for compliments?" said Darcy with a smile, leaning forwards to peer into her face.

Then, more seriously, he went on:

"As a matter of fact, it's not extraordinary to remember the happiest moments of one's life."

"How good you are at acting charades!" said Julie, afraid the conversation might take too sentimental a turn.

"Would you like me to give you another proof of my memory?" interrupted Darcy. "Do you remember our pact at Mme Lambert's? We had sworn to be nasty to everybody but always to support each other against everyone else. But it went the way of most pacts; it was never implemented…"

"How do you know it wasn't?"

"Well, I fancy you didn't get much chance of defending me once I'd left Paris, because who was going to have time to bother about me?"

"Not of defending you, I agree… But of talking about you to your friends."

"My friends!" exclaimed Darcy with rather a rueful smile.

"I hardly had any at that time, at any rate hardly any that you knew. The young men whom your mother knew hated me, why, I don't know; and as for the women, they didn't have much time for a mere attaché in the Ministry of Foreign Affairs."

"That was because you didn't trouble about them."

"That's true. I've never been able to be agreeable to people I couldn't stand."

Had it been possible to see Julie's face in the dark, Darcy would have been able to see a deep blush spread over her features at this last remark, which she interpreted in a way Darcy had not intended.

However, Julie abandoned these reminiscences which were so fresh in both their memories and tried to bring the subject round to his travels in the hope of leaving the conversation to Darcy. This technique is usually very successful with travellers, particularly those from distant parts.

"What a wonderful trip you must have had," she said, "and how sorry I am never to be likely to make one like it."

But Darcy was no longer in a mood for travellers' tales.

"Who was that young man with the moustache?" he asked abruptly. "The one who was talking to you at the party."

This time, Julie blushed even more deeply.

"He's a friend of my husband's," she replied, "an officer from his regiment… They say," she went on, determined to stick to the theme of the East, "that once you have seen that lovely blue sky you can't settle down anywhere else."

"I don't know why," said Darcy, "but I took a great dislike... I mean to your husband's friend, not to the blue sky. But as a matter of fact, as far as the blue sky is concerned, Heaven forbid you should ever have to bear it yourself! You come to loathe it so much, seeing it always the same every day that you really pine for a nasty Paris fog. Believe me, nothing is so nerve-racking as seeing that lovely blue sky and knowing that it will be as blue tomorrow as it was yesterday. If you only knew how desperately you long to see a cloud!"

"And yet you spent a long time under that blue sky!"

"There was nothing much I could do about it. If I had been allowed to do what I wanted, I should have come straight back to the neighbourhood of the rue de Bellechasse as soon as I had satisfied the itch of curiosity which one can't help feeling for the mystery of the East."

"I think a lot of travellers would say the same if they were all as honest as you... How did you pass the time in Constantinople and the other towns?"

"Like everywhere else, there are all sorts of ways of killing time. The English take to drink, the French to gambling, the Germans to smoking and a few more ingenious people, to add a spice of variety, climb on roofs to look at the local women and get themselves shot at."

"I suppose that was your favourite pursuit?"

"Not at all, I spent my time studying Turkish and Greek, which made everyone laugh at me. After I'd finished the Embassy dispatches, I used to go out sketching or have a gallop to the Golden Horn and then go down to the sea-front to see if there weren't some civilized visitors arriving from France or somewhere."

"It must have been very exciting to see a Frenchman such a long way from France."

"Yes, it was, but for one intelligent person, what a lot of junk-merchants and shawl-dealers we used to see! Or what was worse, young poets who, as soon as they saw someone from the Embassy in the offing, started clamouring: Do take me to see the ruins or Saint Sophia or the mountains or the *wine-dark* sea; or I *must* see the spot where Hero used to sit and pine for Leander. Then, when they'd managed to get a touch of the sun, they would shut themselves up in their bedroom and refuse to do anything but read old numbers of their favourite newspaper."

"You see the unpleasant side of everything, as you always did. You haven't changed a bit, you know! You're still as cynical as ever."

"But don't you think that a lost soul frizzling in boiling oil has the right to have a little fun at the expense of his companions in misfortune? Honestly, you don't know how wretched our life is out there. We Embassy secretaries are just birds of passage.

We can't have any of that personal intimacy which makes life worth living… I imagine." These last words were spoken in rather a peculiar tone and he edged a little towards Julie. "For the last six years I've had literally no one to share my thoughts with."

"But didn't you have any friends out there?"

"I've just told you that it's impossible in a foreign country. I'd left two friends behind me in France. One of them is dead and the other is in South America and won't be back for years and then only if he doesn't die of yellow fever before."

"So you're quite alone?"

"Quite alone."

"But what about the women in the East? Didn't their company offer any consolation?"

"But that's the worst of all. As far as Turkish women are concerned, it's quite out of the question. Greeks and Armenians, well, the best you can say about them is that they're very pretty. As for the consuls' and ambassadors' wives, you must excuse me if I don't mention them. It's a question of diplomacy and if I said what I thought, it might do me harm at the Ministry."

"You don't seem to like your career very much. You used to long to become a diplomat!"

"I didn't know what sort of job it was then! Now, I think I'd like to be an inspector of Paris dustmen!"

"Good heavens, how can you say that? Paris! The dullest place on earth!"

"Don't be blasphemous! I should like to hear your opinion after living a couple of years in Naples."

"I'd like to see Naples more than any other place in the world," she sighed, "providing, of course, I had my friends with me."

"Oh, with that proviso, I'm ready to go round the world. Travelling with one's friends! It would be like sitting in your own drawing room watching the world spread out in front of your window like a panorama."

"Well, if I'm asking too much, I should like only one, no, just two friends."

"I don't want as much. One would be enough – male or female," he added with a smile. "But it's something I've never been lucky enough to have... and never shall be," he went on, sighing. Then, more cheerfully, "As a matter of fact, I've always had bad luck. There were only two things I ever really wanted and I never managed to have either of them."

"What were they?"

"Oh, nothing out of the way. One was that I passionately wanted to be able to waltz with someone. I went into the whole problem of waltzing very thoroughly. I practised for months, alone, with a chair to help me from feeling dizzy as I always did and when I at last managed not to be giddy..."

"And who was it you wanted to waltz with?"

"Suppose I said it was you?... And when, after all this effort, I had at last become a perfect waltzer, then your grandmother, who had just started going to a Jansenist confessor, issued a ban on waltzing which I still can't forgive her for."

"And your other wish?" asked Julie, deeply stirred.

"I'll tell you. I wanted – of course, I was asking far too much – I wanted someone to love me... really love me. This was before the question of waltzing. I'm not keeping to the chronological order. I wanted, as I said, to be loved by a woman who preferred my company... to going to a dance – you know, that's really the most serious rival, a ball. A woman whom I could have called on in muddy boots just as she was getting into her carriage to go dancing. She would have been all dressed for the ball and she would have said: I won't go, I'd sooner stay with you. But it was sheer madness. We should only ask for things that are in the realms of possibility!"

"How unkind you are! You're always making cynical remarks and you haven't a good word to say about anything. It's terrible what you say about women."

"Me? Heaven forbid! I'm really blaming myself. Is it terrible to say that a woman would sooner go to a splendid dance than spend the evening alone with me?"

"A splendid dance! Dressed for the ball! Who wants to go dancing these days?"

She was not really trying to defend her sex against Darcy's charges but she thought she understood his hidden meaning, whereas she was, in fact, merely following the dictates of her own heart.

"Talking of dresses and dances, what a shame that carnival's over! I've brought back a charming Greek costume which would suit you admirably."

"You must make a sketch of it in my album."

"I'd love to. You'll be able to see how much I've improved since I used to make funny drawings of people on your mother's tea-table. By the way, I forgot to congratulate you: they told me at the Ministry this morning that your husband was going to be appointed gentleman-in-waiting. I was very pleased."

In spite of herself, Julie gave a start.

Darcy went on without noticing anything:

"You must let me ask you straight away to take me under your wing... But as a matter of fact, I'm not so frightfully pleased at your new dignity... I'm afraid that you may have to go and live at St Cloud during the summer months and so I shan't have the privilege of seeing so much of you."

"I shall never go to St Cloud," said Julie, in a voice full of emotion.

"Oh, so much the better, because, you know, Paris is really a sort of paradise which you should only leave just occasionally for dinner in the country with Mme Lambert, always remembering to come back at night... How lucky you are to be living in Paris! I'm probably only going to be there for a short time, but you can't imagine how pleased I am in the little flat my aunt has given me. And you live in the Faubourg St Honoré, don't you? Someone pointed your house out to me. You must have a charming garden, if all the new building hasn't already turned it into shops?"

"No, my garden's still intact, thank goodness."

"When are you at home?"

"I'm in almost every evening. I shall be delighted if you can find time to come and see me sometimes."

"You see, I'm still behaving as if our old alliance still stands. I'm inviting myself very unceremoniously and even without being officially introduced. You do forgive me, don't you? You are really the only person I know in Paris, apart from Mme Lambert. Everyone else has forgotten me but anyway yours were the only two houses I missed during my exile. I'm sure your parties must be really delightful. You used to choose your friends so well! Do you remember all the plans you used to make in readiness for the time when you would have your own home to be mistress in? A drawing room from which all bores were strictly banned; a little music now and again, but all the time plenty of good conversation, going on till the early hours; nobody pretentious, but a select circle where everybody knows everybody else so that no one needs to lie or show off... Add two or three intelligent women (your friends can't possibly be anything else) and your house must certainly be the nicest in Paris. Yes, I'm sure you're the happiest of women and you must make all those who know you happy, too."

While Darcy was speaking, Julie was thinking to herself that had she married someone else, she might have known the happiness which he was describing so eloquently; had she married Darcy, for example. Instead of this imaginary drawing room, so elegant and agreeable, she thought of all the bores that Chaverny had brought to the house. Instead of sparkling conversation, she recalled all the quarrels between herself and her husband, such as the one which had brought her to P***. And last of all, she saw that she would never be anything else but unhappy, tied for life to a man she hated and despised, whilst the man whom she felt most attracted to in the whole world and whom, without hesitation, she would have trusted to make her happy, was bound to remain a stranger for ever. It was her duty to keep out of his way, to have nothing to do with him and yet he was sitting so close to her that the sleeves of her dress were being crushed by his lapels.

Darcy continued for some time depicting the attractions of life in Paris with all the enthusiasm of someone who had long been without them. Julie felt tears running down her cheeks.

She was terrified that Darcy would notice but her attempt to control her emotions only made them more overpowering. She could scarcely breathe but did not dare to move. Suddenly, a sob broke from her and all was lost. She sank her head into her hands, half choking with tears and shame.

Darcy was taken quite unawares and for a moment astonishment left him speechless; but as the sobs increased, he felt bound to ask the reason for this sudden fit of weeping.

"What's the matter? Please, please answer me! What has happened?"

And as poor Julie, in reply to all his questions, only pressed her handkerchief more tightly to her eyes, he took her hand and gently pulled the handkerchief aside:

"I implore you," he said in an unsteady voice that went straight to Julie's heart, "I implore you to tell me what's wrong. Have I unwittingly said something to hurt you? Please, I can't bear you not to speak."

"Oh dear!" exclaimed Julie, unable to restrain herself any longer, "I'm so unhappy."

"Unhappy? How? Why? What makes you unhappy? Tell me."

So saying, he squeezed her hand, his head almost touching Julie's; but instead of replying she went on weeping. Darcy did not know what to think but he was touched by her tears. He felt six years younger and he began to suspect that at some future date, not yet fixed, he might find himself promoted from the role of confidant to a more important part.

As Julie persisted in not replying, Darcy, afraid that she was going to faint, lowered one of the carriage windows, undid the ribbons of her hat and loosened her coat and scarf… Men are awkward at this sort of operation. He thought of stopping the carriage and he was just going to call out to the driver when Julie seized hold of his arm and begged him not to stop, saying that she felt much better. The coachman had heard nothing and continued to drive on towards Paris.

"I do beg of you, dear Mme de Chaverny," said Darcy, taking her hand again, "I implore you to tell me what's wrong. I'm afraid… I can't understand how I've been unfortunate enough to hurt your feelings."

"Oh, it's not you!" cried Julie, gently squeezing his hand.

"Well then, please tell me what is making you cry like this. Please trust me. Aren't we old friends?" he added, pressing her hand in turn.

"You were talking about all my supposed happiness… and I'm not happy at all!"

"What? Haven't you got everything to make a person happy? You're young, rich, pretty… Your husband holds a very distinguished position…"

"I loathe him!" cried Julie, beside herself. "I loathe and despise him!"

And she hid her head in her handkerchief once more, sobbing more loudly than ever.

"Oho!" thought Darcy. "The plot thickens…"

And he adroitly made use of the jolting of the carriage to edge still closer to the unhappy Julie.

"Why," he murmured as gently and tenderly as possible, "why distress yourself like this? Why worry so much about someone whom you despise? Why let him destroy your happiness? Is he the only person who can make you happy?"

And he kissed her finger-tips; but she immediately withdrew her hand, terrified, and he was afraid that he had gone too far… But being determined to see the affair through to the end, he said, with a rather hypocritical sigh:

"How mistaken I was! When I heard of your marriage, I thought you were really fond of M. de Chaverny."

"Ah, but you never understood me!"

Her tone said quite plainly: I've always loved you and you ignored it. Indeed, the poor woman believed, at that moment, and with the greatest possible sincerity, that for the whole of the last six years she had always loved Darcy as much as she loved him at that instant.

"But how about you?" exclaimed Darcy forcefully. "Did you ever really try to understand me? Did you ever know what my feelings were? Perhaps if you had understood me better, we should both be happier than we are."

"Oh, I'm so unhappy," repeated Julie with a fresh flood of tears, tightly clasping his hand.

"But even if you had understood me," Darcy went on, with his familiar expression of melancholy irony, "what would have been the result? I was without a penny; you were wealthy; your mother would have turned me down as beneath her notice. It was hopeless for me. Yes, and even you, Julie, before you'd learnt from bitter experience what true happiness is, I expect you'd have laughed at my impertinence. I think the only sure key to your affections then was a lovely glossy carriage with a coat-of-arms on the door!"

"Oh God, you too! Won't anyone take pity on me?"

"Oh, forgive me, Julie dear," he cried, himself suddenly moved. "Forgive me and forget those unkind remarks. You're right, it's not for me to blame you, because I'm more to blame than you... I didn't see your true qualities, I thought that you were weak like the other women of your set. I doubted your courage, dear Julie, and I've been badly punished for it!"

Now he was feverishly kissing her hands and she was no longer resisting; he was about to take her in his arms... but in sudden terror, Julie pushed him away and moved to the furthermost edge of the seat. At this Darcy, in a gentle voice which only made the remark more biting, said:

"Excuse me, Mme de Chaverny, I was forgetting that we're in Paris. But now I remember that there, it's marriage which is important, not love."

"Oh, but I do love you!" she whispered, sobbing; and her head sank on to Darcy's shoulder.

Darcy clasped her passionately in his arms and tried to dry her tears with kisses. She made one more attempt to free herself from his arms; but this effort was her last.

12

I T MUST BE OBSERVED that Darcy was mistaken as to the nature of his feelings: he was not in love. He had merely seized his chance of plucking from the tree a fruit that seemed ready to fall into his lap and which was certainly too good to be missed. Moreover, like all men, he was better at asking than thanking. All the same, he was well-mannered and good manners can often replace more reputable feelings. So, once the first ecstasy was over, he delivered himself of a few tender phrases which he composed without too much trouble and which he interspersed with a good deal of hand-kissing, thereby saving himself an equivalent number of words. He was not sorry to see that the carriage was already nearing the gates of Paris and that he was shortly to part company with his conquest. Mme de Chaverny's silence amidst all his protestations of love, the dejection into which she seemed plunged, made her new lover's situation rather difficult and even, if one may be allowed to say so, somewhat tiresome.

She sat motionless in a corner of the carriage, mechanically clutching her shawl to her breast. She had stopped crying; her eyes were staring and whenever Darcy took her hand to kiss it, as soon as he released it, it fell back lifelessly onto her lap. She did not say a word nor did she hear what was being said: but a host of heart-rending thoughts went racing through her brain and as soon as she tried to express one of them, another one would immediately thrust it from her mind.

How can we describe the complete chaos of her thoughts or rather of the images which followed each other as fast as the pounding of her heart? She seemed to hear disconnected, incoherent words that all added up, however, to one dreadful meaning. That morning she had accused her husband and condemned him as a monster; and now she herself was a hundred times more contemptible. In her imagination, her shameless conduct seemed to have become public property: it was the turn of the Duke of H***'s mistress to spurn her now. Mme Lambert and all her friends would never want to see her again. And what of Darcy? Did he love her? He hardly knew her. Had not he forgotten? He had not even recognized her immediately. Perhaps he had found her greatly changed? And now he was cold towards her: this was the final blow. She had been infatuated with a man who scarcely knew her, who had not even shown her any love but merely politeness. It was impossible for him to love her. And did she really love him? No, because she had married someone else almost as soon as he had gone away.

As the carriage drove into Paris, the clocks were striking one o'clock. She had seen Darcy for the first time at four. Yes, seen him – she could hardly say seen him again... She had forgotten his features, his voice: he was a stranger... And nine hours later, she had become his mistress! Nine hours had been enough to cast such a strange spell over her and make her ashamed in her own eyes and in his: for what must he be thinking of a woman who had shown herself so weak? How could he help despising her?

Now and then, the softness of Darcy's voice and his expressions of tenderness revived her hope. In those moments she tried her best to believe that he really felt all the love he was expressing. After all, she hadn't given herself without a struggle. They had loved each other long before Darcy had gone away. Darcy must realize that she had only married out of spite because he had left her. It was all his fault. Yet he had gone on loving her all the time he had been away and when he came back, he had been glad to find that she had not stopped loving him either. Her frank confession, her very weakness must have appealed to Darcy who loathed any sort of deceit. But the absurdity of all this reasoning quickly became plain. All these consoling thoughts melted away and left her in the grip of shame and despair.

Suddenly she felt the need to express what she felt. She had just realized that she was a social outcast, that her family would cast her off; and after all the harm she had done her husband, she would be too proud ever to see him again. "Darcy loves me," she said to herself, "and I can never love anyone but him. I can't be happy without him but with him I can be happy anywhere. Why can't we go away together to some place where I shall never meet anyone to remind me of my disgrace? Why shouldn't he take me to Constantinople?..."

Darcy was very far from guessing what was going on in Julie's heart. He had just noticed that they were entering the street where Mme de Chaverny lived and started pulling on his gloves with great composure:

"Incidentally," he said, "I must be officially introduced to M. de Chaverny. I imagine we shall soon become good friends. With an introduction from Mme Lambert, I shall have a good start in your house. In the meantime, as he's in the country, may I come and see you?"

Julie was struck dumb. Every word he uttered was like a dagger thrust into her heart. How could she talk of eloping, of running away to a man so calm, so cold, who was only thinking about the best way to organize a convenient little liaison for the summer? In her rage, she snapped the gold charm round her neck and twisted its links between her fingers. The carriage stopped in front of her door. Darcy was most solicitous in arranging her shawl round her shoulders and helping her to put her hat straight. When the carriage door was opened, he offered her his hand with a most respectful air, but Julie leapt down without accepting his help.

"I shall ask you, Mme de Chaverny," he said with a low bow, "to let me call on you and enquire how you are."

"Goodbye," said Julie in a choking voice.

Darcy climbed back into his carriage and was carried off home whistling like a man who has done a good day's work.

13

As soon as he got back to his bachelor flat, Darcy slipped on his Turkish dressing gown, put his slippers on and, filling the white amber bowl of his long cherry-wood pipe with best-cut Turkish tobacco, he settled down to enjoy it, sprawling in a large well-upholstered morocco-leather easy-chair. If you are surprised to see him enjoying such a vulgar occupation at a time when he should perhaps be indulging in more poetic thoughts, I can only reply that a pipe of good tobacco is a useful, if not indeed an essential adjunct to dreaming and that the right way to enjoy something properly is to combine it with other forms of enjoyment. One of my friends, a great voluptuary, would never open a letter from his mistress without first having taken off his tie, poked up the fire if it was in winter and stretched out on a comfortable settee.

"I must admit," meditated Darcy, "that I should have been a fool to take Tyrrel's advice and buy a little Greek slave-girl to bring back to Paris with me. It would have been like taking figs to Damascus, as my friend Haleb Effendi would say. Thank goodness that civilization has made great strides while

I've been away and moral rectitude doesn't seem to be too much over-emphasized. Poor old Chaverny! Well, if I'd had enough money a few years ago, I should have married Julie and perhaps it might have been Chaverny who would have brought her home this evening. If I ever marry, I shall take good care to have my wife's carriage overhauled frequently so that she doesn't need any knight errant to pull her out of ditches... Now, let's think. All things considered, she's a very pretty woman and no fool and if I were a bit younger than I am, I might easily imagine that it's because of my outstanding qualities... My outstanding qualities, indeed! Unfortunately in a month's time, my outstanding qualities will be about the same as those of the man with the moustache... My God, I wish that my little Nastasia had only been able to read and write and talk with educated people, because I was very fond of her and I think she's the only woman who's ever really loved me. Poor little thing!..." His pipe went out and he soon dropped off to sleep.

14

GOING INTO HER ROOM, Mme de Chaverny mustered all her strength and told her maid as naturally as she could that she wasn't needed and could go. As soon as the girl had gone, she flung herself on to her bed and, now that she was alone, started weeping even more bitterly than when Darcy's presence had restrained her.

There is no doubt that night has a most powerful effect on moral suffering as well as on physical pain. It casts a shadow over everything and thoughts that would be considered quite normal, or even pleasant in daytime, worry and torment us at night like ghosts that come out only in the dark. At night the mind seems doubly active and reason loses all its power. A kind of hallucination fills our minds with worry and fright and makes us incapable either of ridding ourselves of our fears or examining them objectively.

So poor Julie lay half-undressed on her bed, tossing restlessly to and fro, alternately burning with fever and shivering with icy cold, starting at the slightest creak in the woodwork, her heart-beats pounding in her ears. All she remembered about her situation was a vague feeling of dread which she vainly tried to explain to herself. Then all at once the memory of that fatal evening returned and with it an agonizing pain which pierced her brain like a red-hot dagger in a wound.

Sometimes she stared stupidly at the flickering of the flame, until the tears which welled up in her eyes, without her knowing why, prevented her from seeing the light.

"What are all these tears for?" she asked herself. "Oh, I'm dishonoured!"

Then she would count the tassels on the curtains round her bed but she could never remember how many there were.

"Am I out of my mind?" she thought. "Out of my mind? Yes, because only an hour ago I gave myself like a miserable prostitute to a man I didn't know."

Then she stared vacantly at the hand of the clock, as anxiously as a condemned man waiting to be taken to the place of execution. Suddenly the clock struck.

"Three hours ago," she said, starting up convulsively, "I was with him and now I am dishonoured!"

She passed the whole night in this fever of agitation. When day appeared, she opened her window and the sharp, fresh morning air somewhat relieved her. Leaning over the balustrade of her window which overlooked the garden, she breathed in the cold air with almost a sensual pleasure. Gradually her thoughts became calmer. Her vague torment and delirium were succeeded by a concentrated despair that was a relief in comparison.

She had to take a decision and she started to think what was to be done. Not for a moment did she consider whether to see Darcy again. It seemed to her impossible; she would have died of shame at the mere sight of him. She must leave Paris, where everybody would soon be pointing the finger of scorn at her. Her mother was at Nice; she would join her there and confess everything; then, having opened her heart to her, there was only one thing more to do and that was to find some deserted spot in Italy off the beaten track, and live there alone in the hope that she might die as soon as possible.

Once she had made this resolution, she felt calmer. She sat down at a little table in front of her window and wept with her head in her hands, but this time without bitterness. Fatigue and prostration finally had their way and she went to sleep or, at least, ceased to think for about an hour.

She woke up shivering and feverish. The weather had changed, the sky was grey and an icy drizzle promised cold and damp for the rest of the day. Julie rang for her maid.

"My mother's ill," she told her. "I must leave for Nice without delay. Pack a trunk, I want to go in an hour from now."

"But madam, what's the matter? Are you ill? You haven't been to bed!" exclaimed the maid, surprised and alarmed at the change in her mistress.

107

"I must go," said Julie impatiently. "It's absolutely necessary. Get my trunk ready."

In our modern civilization, the mere desire is not enough to move from one place to another: things have to be wrapped up, cardboard boxes have to be filled and a hundred other things done which almost take away the desire to leave. But Julie was so impatient that many of these inevitable delays were shortened. She went to and fro from room to room, helping to pack the trunks herself, throwing in dresses and hats which were unused to such careless treatment. The result of this activity was, of course, to hinder rather than help her servants.

"Has madam told the master?" asked the maid timidly.

Julie did not reply but took a piece of paper and wrote: *My mother is ill in Nice. I'm going to see her.* She folded the paper across but found herself incapable of writing the address.

In the midst of these preparations for the journey, a servant came in:

"M. de Châteaufort is enquiring if he can see madam," he said. "There is also another gentleman who came in at the same time whom I don't know. Here is his card."

She read: *M. Darcy. Secretary to the Embassy.*

"I'm not in for anyone," she exclaimed. "Say I'm ill but don't say I'm going away."

She could not explain why Châteaufort and Darcy both happened to call on her at the same time and, distraught as she was, she imagined that Darcy must already have confided in Châteaufort. Nothing was simpler, in fact, than their simultaneous appearance. Bent on the same errand, they had met at the door and having exchanged a very cool "Good afternoon", they had each, privately but wholeheartedly, sent the other to hell. On receiving the servant's reply, they both went down the steps together, said goodbye to each other more distantly than ever and went off in opposite directions.

Châteaufort had noticed the particular attention Mme de Chaverny had paid Darcy and, from that moment, had taken a dislike to him. For his part, Darcy, who prided himself on being a judge of faces, had only needed to observe Châteaufort's embarrassment and arrogance to conclude that he was in love with Julie and since, being a diplomat, he was always ready to assume the worst, he had made up his mind, most irresponsibly, that Julie was Châteaufort's mistress.

"What a strange little flirt she is," he said to himself on his way out. "She didn't want to receive us together for fear of a scene. But I was an idiot not to find some excuse for staying behind and letting that conceited young puppy go off alone. I'm sure that if I had only waited until his back was turned, I should have been allowed in, because there's no doubt that I have at least the advantage of novelty over him."

While musing thus, he stopped, turned back and went into Mme de Chaverny's house once more.

Châteaufort who had looked round several times, retraced his steps and stationed himself some distance away to keep watch on Darcy.

The servant was surprised to see Darcy again. Darcy explained that he had an urgent message to Mme de Chaverny from one of her friends. Remembering that Julie knew English, he pencilled on his card: *Ventures to ask when he can show Mme de Chaverny his Turkish album.* He handed the card to the servant and said he would wait for the reply.

The reply was long in coming. Finally, the servant came back very flustered and said:

"Mme de Chaverny has just fainted and is not well enough to give an answer at the moment."

All this had taken a quarter of an hour. Darcy did not really believe in the fainting but it was plain that he was not going to be admitted. He resigned himself philosophically and remembering that he had some calls to make in the neighbourhood, he left unperturbed by this slight hitch.

Châteaufort was waiting in a frenzy of anxiety for him to come out. When he saw him go by, he suddenly felt certain that his rival was successful and he promised himself to seize the first opportunity of revenging himself on the faithless Julie and her aider and abettor. He confided his fears to Major

Perrin, who appeared most opportunely at this moment. The Major consoled him as best he could by pointing out how unlikely all his suspicions were.

15

I N FACT, JULIE HAD REALLY FAINTED on seeing Darcy's second card. When she came to, she began to spit blood, which made her extremely weak. Her maid sent for her doctor but Julie stubbornly refused to see him. At about four o'clock, the post-horses arrived and the trunks were loaded up. Everything was ready for the departure. Julie was lifted into the carriage, coughing horribly and in a pitiful state. Throughout the evening and night, she only spoke to the footman sitting up on the driver's seat and then merely to tell the postilions to drive faster. She was racked by a continual cough and seemed to have great pain in her chest; but she made not the slightest complaint. In the morning, she was so feeble that she fainted when the carriage-door was opened. They stopped at a miserable little country inn and put her to bed. The village doctor was sent for. He found that she had a very high fever and forbade her to go on. In the evening, she became delirious and her symptoms became much graver. She talked all the time and so volubly that it was difficult to follow her. In her disjointed phrases, the names of Darcy,

Châteaufort and Mme Lambert appeared again and again. The maid wrote off to M. de Chaverny to tell him of his wife's illness; but she was almost a hundred miles from Paris, while Chaverny was shooting at the Duke of H***'s and the illness was developing so rapidly that he was unlikely to arrive in time.

Meanwhile the footman had ridden over to the neighbouring town to fetch a doctor, who criticized his colleague's treatment, pointed out that they'd delayed a long time before calling him and stated that the illness was a serious one.

At daybreak, the delirium ceased and Julie fell into a deep sleep. When she woke up, two or three days later, she seemed to find it difficult to remember by what series of accidents she found herself in bed in the dirty inn-room. However, her memory soon returned. She said she felt better and even talked of leaving the next day. Then, after seeming to reflect for a long time with her hand on her forehead, she asked for paper and ink and tried to write. Her maid watched her begin letters which she kept on tearing up after the first few words. At the same time, she gave instructions for all the torn pieces of paper to be burnt. The maid noticed on a number of the scraps of paper the word: *Monsieur*. This, she said, seemed very strange, for she thought that madam was writing to her mother or her husband. On one fragment, she read: *You must thoroughly despise me…*

For almost half an hour, she tried in vain to write the letter which seemed to be causing her so much concern. In the end, she was too exhausted to continue; she pushed away the writing table on her bed and said, bewildered:

"Write to M. Darcy yourself."

"What am I to write, madam?" enquired the maid, convinced that Julie was becoming delirious again.

"Tell him that he doesn't understand me... that I can't understand him..."

She fell back exhausted on her pillow.

This was her last coherent utterance. She fell into a delirium from which she never recovered. She died the following day, without seeming to suffer greatly.

16

C HAVERNY ARRIVED three days after her funeral. His grief seemed sincere and all the inhabitants of the village wept as he stood in the graveyard looking at the fresh mound of earth covering his wife's coffin. At first, he wanted her to be exhumed and taken back to Paris; but as the mayor objected and the lawyer spoke of endless complications, he merely gave instructions to erect a simple but appropriate tombstone.

Châteaufort was much affected by her extremely sudden death. He refused several invitations to dances and for some time wore only black.

Amongst Julie's friends, there were various versions of her death. Some said that she had a dream, or, if you like, a strange foreboding that her mother was ill. She was so deeply impressed by this that she at once set out for Nice in spite of having a bad cold which she had caught coming back from Mme Lambert's and this cold had turned into inflammation of the lungs.

Others, more discerning, asserted in mysterious tones that Mme de Chaverny, no longer able to ignore her love for M. de

Châteaufort, had turned to her mother for help. The cold and pneumonia were the consequence of her hurried departure. On this last point, there was agreement.

Darcy never mentioned her name. Three or four months after her death, he made a *good* marriage. When he announced it to Mme Lambert, she congratulated him and added: "You've a really charming wife and only my poor Julie would have suited you as well. What a pity you hadn't enough money at the time when she married."

Darcy gave his usual ironical smile but made no reply.

These two people who had so misunderstood each other were perhaps made for one another.

ONEWORLD CLASSICS

ONEWORLD CLASSICS aims to publish mainstream and lesser-known European classics in an innovative and striking way, while employing the highest editorial and production standards. By way of a unique approach the range offers much more, both visually and textually, than readers have come to expect from contemporary classics publishing.

To order any of our titles and for up-to-date information about our current and forthcoming publications, please visit our website on:

www.oneworldclassics.com